NOVOCAINE

Novel by David Kanellis

Story by Michael Kanellis

TABLE OF CONTENTS

Acknowledgements

This book is dedicated to Amy who tolerated several questionable dental procedures while I was in dental school, and to Nick and Alex who played countless hours of Nintendo with their grandfather.

PROLOGUE

In 1982 I was roommates with Rob Watzke at 14 ½ S. Clinton Street in Iowa City, Iowa. I had just finished my residency in Pediatric Dentistry and Rob was a senior at the University of Iowa majoring in film. I shared a story with Rob that I thought would make a great movie. The plot involved a dentist who needed money and a friend in the mafia who needed a favor. The name of the movie was to be "Novocaine". Rob encouraged me to work on a screenplay for the movie.

One Sunday while having dinner with my parents I shared my movie idea with my dad, David Kanellis. He suggested I should consider writing a novel before turning it into a screenplay. He was interested in hearing the details, and I left him with my screenplay outline and all my notes. Then time passed.

Rob graduated from the University and moved to Los Angeles. I continued in private practice in Muscatine, Iowa, got married to my wife Amy, and had two sons, Nicholas, and Alex. On Christmas Eve in 1989, we were at my parent's house to open presents. I unwrapped a gift from my dad and was stunned to find that it was the completed novel "Novocaine" typed on 8 ½ X 11 sheets of white paper. I really could not believe it.

Over the next several days I read and reread the novel. I was initially somewhat disappointed that instead of creating an edge-of-your-seat thriller (which I had intended), my dad had turned my story into a comedy-drama along the lines of "The World According to Garp". In hindsight, I am embarrassed that I failed to recognize his genius in doing so. His semi-autobiographical approach, drawing on so many of his own life experiences and obsessions, made for a much more entertaining read. I hope you enjoy it.

—Mike Kanellis

Chapter 1

The Reunion

Willard Mosley maneuvered his way across three lanes of traffic in his rented Dodge Dynasty and swung right at the toll road, the invitation to the class reunion pinned to the visor, wondering why he was bothering to make the trip. Especially without Karen. A month before, when the invitation arrived in the office mail, he was so certain Karen would go along with the idea that he had bought two airline tickets to Cedar Rapids for the 4th of July.

"Willie," she had said, as she left the house for her aerobics class, "you know it's out of the question. The Elmhurst chapter of the 'Elvis Presley Lives' Club is going to Graceland the 4th of July weekend, and that is where I will be. Besides that, I have zero in common with anyone in your class at SUI high school. I don't even go to my own class reunions at Skokie."

The way she said "SUI" sounded more like the grunt of a runt pig than the traditional hog calling squeal of the old crowds at SUI high school football games. Before they closed the school, that is. But Will thought it futile to pursue the topic. Their marriage had sort of fallen apart after the first two years, but they had remained together for a total of 14 years come November, partly because he thought he still loved her, but mostly because a divorce now would merely complicate his problems.

Despite the fact that Karen was outspending his annual income from his dental office in the shopping center, he truly believed he was better off with her than without. Nor did she begin to comprehend their financial status. He was nearly two years in arrears to the IRS, no bank would loan him any more money, he had saturated the mortgage capacity on his home, and could not even get anyone to finance a new automobile. The way Willie figured, he needed approximately half a million dollars just to get back to where they were 10 years ago.

"Flat," went through his mind as the toll road narrowed to two lanes. Illinois had to be the flattest place in the world, but you had to be well out of Chicago's skyscrapers to notice. "Illinois is flat and I am flat . . . broke that is," he told himself as he found a Cubs game on the radio. A typical Cubs season closely paralleled Will's marriage. Starting out with hope, ending with excuses and long losing streaks, while yet pretending everything was going well.

"Good God," he said as he heard the announcer say, 'Maddox will face the latter third of the batting order this inning.' "It's no wonder athletes and sports fans are illiterate . . . if you have 'latter third,' then there must have been a 'former third' leaving another third of the nine players unaccounted for." Will could easily forgive Dizzy Dean's language butchery, because Dean's mistakes had been real, just like those of his own Medicaid dental patients, but what he could not bear was garbage language intended to be sophisticated, such as hearing a Midwesterner pronounce the first syllable of "either" and "neither" to rhyme with "my" instead of the natural "me." And no ball player, coach or announcer would ever say "me" when they could substitute the incorrect "I" or "myself," such as "Steve and myself will be signing autographs at Harry's restaurant this evening." Or, "This is just between you and I, Steve."

Will wondered if he should have been a sports announcer instead of a dentist. He fondly remembered Old Man Smitherman, his English teacher at SUI high and believed he actually learned something there. True, most of the SUI students, if they thought at all, believed their teachers were sent from the University to SUI high as punishment for not publishing. Or more likely, for not politicking. "Publish, politick, or perish," the University's inner-circle dictum read, and the nonorthodox were sent over to SUI High to teach them a lesson. As a result, Will's entire high school education had been provided by doddering old men, supplemented with aspiring student teachers, whose main mission in the 60's was to assure the SUI students that unlike the old men, they themselves were cool cats.

But Will had found Smitherman to be neither doddering nor deserving of punishment. His message prevailed whenever Will heard one of those TV meteorologists mention "WHITE STUFF,

WEATHERWISE" or "BEAR GITOUTCHER BRELLAS CUZ AFRUNNEL SYSTEMS COMIN' IN."

Between innings the station broke for a commercial, as Will heard an inarticulate athlete plugging only moderate drinking for teenagers. "Know wen to say 'wen,'" Will heard for the umpteenth time, thinking again of what Old Man Smitherman might have said to SUI students during his day.

"People who say 'Know when to say when,'" Smitherman would have grunted, "don't know how to say 'when'. They say 'wen.'" Then he would light a match, hold it up to his mouth and say "wen. . . wen. . . wen. . . wen," as the fire got closer and closer to his cigarette-stained thumb and finger, while the students watched. Then at the last second he would aspirate a loud "when" at the fire, which promptly went out. Usually when this happened, after a lesson on the difference between "why" and "wye," (the SUI students' most common diction error), a few of the braver kids in the class would shout, "Make a wish, Mr. Smitherman."

The highway sign, painted in the standard shit-brindle brown historical site color, read "Dixon, Home of President Reagan," reminding Will why he was in debt, flat broke, and driving a rented car, paid for by cash (in advance) from his office funds, because the agency would not accept his check. It really wasn't anything Reagan had done, thought Will, because in eight years in the White House no one could nail him down for doing anything at all. It was Nancy.

Will's problems began when Karen started reading about Nancy and watching all the talk shows. For a few years Karen actually tried to be Nancy, trying to match her weight pound for pound, and her wardrobe expenses, dollar-for-dollar. She did quite well on the dollar-for-dollar part, too, for that matter, considering Will was taking in only $200,000 per year. But expensive as Karen's Nancy Reagan days were, her present clothes kick, buying sequined country western outfits, was worse, especially so since her new ambition was to match garment for garment each Elvis Presley costume on display at Graceland in Nashville, where Karen religiously paid homage twice each year.

The last words Will heard as he left the toll road at 4:00 p.m. were "Have a good day." It was a trifle late for that, he thought, as he forked over his $4.20 or whatever it was. These days, anything less than half a million dollars did not mean much, so he didn't really care if the toll charge was $4.20, $42 or $420 dollars. Nothing mattered any more unless he could get hold of some real money, get out of debt, get the IRS off his back and his marriage back together.

As he crossed the Mississippi Will stopped at the first rest stop on I-80 and reread his reunion invitation. Old Man Smitherman would have flunked Kathy Norton for the big smiling face she had made on Will's copy. "Hope you can come - - - smiling face - - - and three exclamation marks." Kathy. In Will's opinion a smiling face was nearly as insulting as to say, "Have a good day." As for the exclamation marks, Smitherman had taught Will to despise them. "I don't want a bunch of alarmists coming out of SUI High," Smitherman would say as he read a student paper peppered with exclamation marks. "Save them for such sentences as 'Help, help, the radicals just blew up the University!' When that happens, and not until then, be satisfied with periods and question marks. For that matter," Smitherman added, "you don't need exclamation marks there. Take a look at the Bible. It tells us that God said, 'Let there be light, and there was light.' If you can find an exclamation mark following all those miracles in the Bible, even the one that says, 'Moses tied his ass to a tree and climbed up the mountain,' show it to me and I'll raise your grade. Also, if you can show me any book," he digressed, "where they dot their I's with circles instead of dots, I will raise your grade for that also."

Free road maps were available in the rest stop, so Will took one as he came out of the men's room. Then seeing a huge bronze sign mentioning area historical events, he thought of Smitherman again. On the bottom of the sign, it said, "Over." "Think of that," he told himself, "who the hell is going to pick up this 900-pound sign and turn it over to read the other side?" If it said "over" on the other side, Will could be reading the sign for the rest of his life. It was like the Polish jokes they had on Chicago's North side. But it did read "over" on the reverse side. Will could visualize a tourist obeying the "over" signs and running back and forth at the rest stop until he got arrested. All for merely obeying instructions.

While finishing the last few miles of the trip Will wondered who all would be at the reunion. And would they say, "Hi, Will," or "Hi, Wormy?" No one had called him "Wormy" for years, and since Chad

Baxter got killed in an auto accident while driving to Canada to avoid the Viet Nam war, only one person, Randy Harrigan, could prove the reason behind the nickname. And if anyone could keep a secret Randy could.

Will remembered sports page headlines of his high school career, "Little Wart Hogs win on Wormy Mosley's 50-yard run," and "Wormy Mosley scores three touchdowns in win over Tipton." SUI High teams were called Little Hogs to distinguish them from another local high school team, going by the name "Little Hawks" in honor of the University team's Hawkeyes. But, as Smitherman had said more than once, "People are too lazy to say 'Hawkeyes' and will pronounce 'Hawks' and 'Hogs' the same anyway, so it really does not matter what you call yourselves."

About the name "Wormy" he remembered sweating it out as he read one write-up, "Wormy got his nickname from (continued on page 4)," and then (thank God), "the way he worms his way through opposing tacklers on his way to the goal line."

The nickname got pinned on Will in the SUI High shower room in 7th grade, when Chad pointed at his ass, leaped from the shower and shouted, "Wormy, Wormy!" as a huge ugly white tapeworm, measuring at least a half inch in diameter and two feet in length, emerged from Will's anal passage. It was the first and only time a thing like that ever happened, because his mother promptly took him to the clinic, where the doctor said Will must have got hold of some bad Halloween candy. Will's mom thought he might have picked up the tapeworm in the lunchroom at SUI high, where decayed food particles in the cracks of the tables dated back to the turn of the century.

But as for Will himself, it didn't matter. He wanted to forget the whole experience, yet he never pulled a tooth without somehow recalling the struggle he and Randy had gone through extracting the tape worm from his ass.

The name "Wormy" caught on among the guys on the football team, but today only Randy could prove the reason. And he would never tell. It is strange about nicknames. An older woman teacher, sent over to SUI High to teach typing when the guys were in 9th grade, had a bit of trouble with the names at first, and often looked Randy straight in the eye, and called him "Dick." Finally, one day he said, "My name is

Randy," to which she replied, "Randy, I'm sorry, but you look like a Dick to me."

So the guys all had a big guffaw, especially Chad, and called him "Dick" after that. All except Will, that is. He never called Randy, "Dick," and Randy never called Will, "Wormy."

As he drove into the parking lot at the College Athletic club, he read, "Welcome, Little Hogs, Class of 1966," without exclamation marks. Somewhat of an improvement over the sign at the west door, which read, "Welcome, West Liberty High Class of 81!!"

Inside the door, in true reunion fashion were two tables, one covered with a stack of old SUI yearbooks, old school papers, play programs; the other with name tags, all in alphabetical order, thanks to the efficient work of Reunion Secretary Kathy Norton and Reunion Treasurer Missy Finch, both sitting behind the tables. Four years of cheerleading at SUI High had prepared them for the organizational details involved in a class reunion. Night after night in high school, you could see them on the floor, coloring long strips of butcher paper, inscribing in square letters, each a different color, such motivational messages as "Pluck the Eagles," "Declaw the Wildcats," or "Sink the Sailors," each message followed by two or three exclamation marks. Add to this Kathy and Missy's Monday task of pasting three-by-five cards on the lockers of each member of the football team, bearing the likes of "Congratulations, Will, beat the Spartans," with a new message each week, but with only the opponent's totem changed, "Congratulations, Will, beat the Tigers." Recycling and forest-saving were not yet discussed at SUI High in 1966.

"Willy!!!" screeched Kathy, as soon as he picked up his name tag, "thanks for coming!!! Let me help you with that!!" Which she did, pulling him toward her by his left lapel, steering him to the side of the table with her left hand. "You don't look a day older, where's? - - -"

"Karen couldn't come. You look the same, too. About Karen. Long story. Talk about it later," he said, not thinking of a satisfactory reason for Karen's not coming to SUI's reunion. "But I wouldn't have missed it for the world."

Kathy wasn't listening to his mumbling anyway, as she turned to two more classmates, who had driven in together from Des Moines, greeting them and giving them the same treatment.

Turning to his left he was pleased to see the back of a head covered with a mass of dark red hair. Only one person had hair that color, his best friend from long ago, Randy Harrigan. It looked hardly different from the back, except for a dollar-pancake-sized bald spot right on top in the middle. He himself still had hair on top in the middle, but it had receded significantly at the front.

If there was one thing Randy did not like it was to be sneaked up on from behind, so Will called his name from a few feet away, "Randy."

"I was hoping you'd be here," said Randy, holding a Scotch on the Rocks. "What'll you have? I'm buying."

"Great, Cutty Sark is all I drink these days, jeeze, it's great to see you. Where are you living now? I lost track of you a few years ago when . ."

"I was sent up. Go ahead and say it. Everybody knows. Actually, Chicago. Been there twelve years, got a wife, four sons and a fifth kid due next week. That's why Jo couldn't come. Her name's Josephine but everyone calls her 'Jo.' Even her old man. Always wanted a son, never had one." Randy pulled out his wallet to show a recent family picture. "Last year's Christmas card," he said. "If I knew where you were, I would have sent you one."

Removing another snapshot from his wallet, Randy proudly announced, "My wife, Jo. That's her good side, there," he said. "Profile. The first time I saw her was at her old man's house and he called her in from the kitchen. Just the two of them lived there. She was real shy. Had a huge birthmark all over the left side of her face. Her old man said, 'Show the young man your good side, Jo,' and she shyly turned showing the same profile you see in the photo. Then he told me, 'Beautiful on one side, hell of a cook, loves kids, best wife anyone could ever have. No one will ever try to take her away from you because they won't see the whole picture. Think it over.'"

"Then what?" Will wanted to know.

"Well, I knew her old man from my bad days, before I was sent to Joliet, and had learned to pretty much follow his advice. It pays, too. That white Cadillac in the parking lot is what I'm driving. Have another just like it."

"Whew," whistled Will, "Where do you live in Chicago? We live in Elmhurst, no kids yet, said Will, Karen won't be here either. Went to Memphis for the weekend."

"Her folks live in Memphis?"

"No, but she thinks Elvis Presley does. Has a whole damn club called 'Elvis Lives.' They're all going to Memphis together. Karen's quite a bit younger than I am and gets around a lot," explained Will.

"Whadya say we go somewhere after the reunion dinner, Will? You're about the only one I really know out of the whole class."

Will agreed, not knowing if Randy really wanted company or if he thought he himself did. Either way, it was better than going with the rest of the class to watch the 4th of July Fireworks at City Park.

Just then a hush filled the reception room as a man from the care center pushed a wheelchair through the door into the room. The occupant of the wheelchair sat with his head slumped over his clavicle, long strands of dirty white hair flowing out in all directions beneath a moth-eaten black stocking cap, actually a U.S. Navy watch cap from World War II. He was wearing the same gabardine navy blue suit he wore when he taught at SUI high, as covered with dandruff as ever. It was the reunion's guest of honor, Old Man Smitherman.

"Jesus," muttered Randy, sipping from his Scotch, "he's still alive."

"Yah, he must be at least 85. He was pushing retirement age when we had him in class." Will continued, "The way I heard the story, after they closed the school and turned it into a warehouse for the University, he worked his way into the school nearly every day, used a walker back then, made his way into our old English classroom and delivered lectures to a roomful of soap and toilet tissue boxes. I remember my mother writing to me shortly before she got killed. She said the chalkboard was still in what was now a storage room and Smitherman had written a lot of paired names on it, like Sacco and Vanzetti, Leopold and Loeb, Troillus and Cressida, Bonnie and Clyde, Antony and Cleopatra. She couldn't remember the rest. She hated it that they used his daily lectures in the storeroom as an excuse to put him away. He's been living in the care center ever since, but I was sure he would be dead by now.

Will well remembered their final term assignment from Smitherman. He said he wanted the class to work in pairs on a term project, and to complete the assignment, each of the 15 pairs of students would write a paper and produce a skit on one of the 15 paired names he had scribbled on the board. Or, as Smitherman had told them, "Because this list is neither prescriptive nor exhaustive, you may choose another pair of names. Come up with two of your own if you wish."

It was one of those days when you remember every detail. There Smitherman was, up at the chalkboard, picking up what he thought was a piece of chalk from the tray to start writing, but he found that it was one of his own cigarette butts instead. Then he looked at the dust-filthy board, picked up an even dustier eraser, and made it only worse. One thing about SUI high, you never had to worry about the janitors erasing important things from the chalkboard overnight, because whatever the teacher wrote on the board was still there until that same teacher erased it, often weeks or even months later. Teachers joked occasionally, that you never had to write "SAVE" on any SUI high chalkboards, because the custodians were State Employees and members of the union.

After tossing the eraser into the wastebasket, Smitherman had said, "This is important," and grossed everybody out by spitting on the heel of his right hand and erasing the dust from the board, about six square inches per spit. Then came the paired names. Will and Randy chose Leopold and Loeb, two Chicago University students who had set out to commit a perfect crime, murdering a young kid and leaving his body in a culvert on Chicago's South Side. The only mistake they made was by Leopold, who had left his eyeglasses beside the victim. A check on the prescription for the glasses led directly to Nathan Leopold.

He also vividly remembered the skit he and Randy had done before the class, re-enacting the crime. While the other students' performances were merely done out of duty, in hoping to get a good grade, Will and Randy had gone all out. Especially Randy, who showed great promise as a make-up artist. Using photographs of Leopold and Loeb, Randy, with a few bundles of hair and lots of grease paint from the Max Factor company, turned Will into Leopold and himself into Loeb. The class loved it, except for three or four of the girls who upon seeing the excellent performance were heard to mutter, "There goes my 'A.' They just did that to make us look bad."

Smitherman had, of course, watched their skit, in addition to reading the papers intensively and called in each pair of students for an hour session after school, telling the two boys that as good as eyeglasses were for identification purposes, dental work was even better. Will found this observation to be very true a few years later when he enrolled in dental school at the University of Iowa. Smitherman also told Randy that he might have a career in stage makeup and offered him a job backstage for their contest one-act play. It was a cutting from the Wizard of Oz, and at the play festival at the university, Randy's Tin Woodsman won top honors in the stage makeup division.

"Mr. Smitherman," Will said to the bowed head as he approached the wheelchair, "I'm Will Mosley. Good to see you."

"You don't have to tell me," Smitherman croaked, raising his head a trifle. "I have forgotten just about everything, but I will never forget the paper you and Randy Harrigan did together. The one on Leopold and Loeb. A hell of a lot better than the ones I got by the kids who didn't understand the assignment, 'Advice and Consent,' 'Frankie and Johnny,' 'War and Peace.' Even 'Julian Dubuque.' Two girls thought the name was 'Julie and Dubuque.' My God, a 6th grader should know better than that," he concluded as his head dropped back to his chest.

"Thanks, Mr. Smitherman. You were a great teacher. Randy is right here too." But Will could have saved his compliment, as Smitherman was fast asleep.

Just then Kathy Norton and Missy Finch, sharing a microphone roaring with feedback, hollered a resounding "SUI, SUI, SUI," which got everyone's attention, after which Kathy announced, "Find your place cards. They are a big surprise, and you'll have to think back. Take the topic you wrote 25 years ago for Mr. Smitherman's paired paper, and that's where you will sit. They say it's time to eat."

Will and Randy found a table for four, labeled "Leopold and Loeb," right next to Jim Collins and Marcy Breakwater who sat at a table for two labeled "Bonnie and Clyde." It was the only table for two in the club, and rightfully so, for they had married each other right out of high school.

Smitherman, with the man from the nursing home standing behind his wheelchair, was seated at the head table with Kathy and Missy, the place card reading, "Tea and Sympathy." Kathy and Missy had been sickened by Smitherman's spitting on his hands at the board when the assignment was made (so they had said) and had missed the point of the assignment. But two weeks later Smitherman told them they could go ahead and do "Tea and Sympathy" as long as they had already started on it. It would never do to read two books the same year, he had wryly observed. The girls agreed and graduated right on time.

"Shall we bow our heads for a silent moment of grace," announced Kathy, amidst the roar of the feedback.

"They ought to turn off that goddam mike," said Randy, "Let's eat and get out of here. I've only got a couple of hours."

"I'm not even hungry," Will said, examining his red cloth napkin. "And they closed the bar."

"There's another one about 100 feet behind this partition," Randy answered. "Let's go there and then come back if we want to."

In the other bar, after two more Scotches and more small talk, Will disclosed to Randy that not all was going well with him, either his marriage or his work. When he said he would be OK if he could borrow about $300,000 to tide him over the next few months and clear him with the IRS, Randy let out a little whistle.

"I've been to every bank in Cook County, plus some of the Chicago suburbs," said Will, "and I simply lack the collateral to float a loan that big. I've even tried to get three or four smaller loans, totaling to three or four hundred thou, but no go."

"There is a way," volunteered Randy, "I am sure I can't help you myself but maybe my father-in-law can. I work for him."

"What kind of work? Sales?"

"Well, sort of like sales. It's really a small family business, and loaning money is part of the business," Randy answered, looking down at the table.

"I mean, what is it you do? Next week, for instance, I will be seeing kids in the dental office from all over the Elmhurst area. Then my office manager, Hilda, will fill out a bunch of forms, and if the state of Illinois is as efficient as ever on those Medicaid claims, I should get paid within a year. What is your typical day like?"

"Well," said Randy, "I'm really into electronics. The family business is called 'AAAA Ltd.' A good name if you want to get in the front of the phone book, and the yellow page ad says, 'Loans, Investments, Trouble Shooting.' I work on mostly the Trouble Shooting aspect and have three Midwestern states as my territory, Iowa, North and South Dakota. Do a lot of driving."

"Tomorrow," continued Randy, "I'm going over to Tama to talk to the Meskwakis about their new Las Vegas-style gambling casino. Then I will head up toward Lake Okoboji to look into some Riverboat Gambling prospects. The next day I continue to Fargo to analyze the cost-effectiveness of a few juke boxes, video games, and possibly a slot machine or two. That's where the electronics comes in, though I shouldn't be telling you any more details."

"When will you be back in Chicago?" asked Will. "I think I am a damned good prospective client for AAAA Ltd. How do I go about getting half a million dollars?"

"I'm not sure you really want to. Our interest rate is a few points higher than most financial institutions. And we always get our money back, no matter what," he said with a furtive grin.

"Afraid I don't have much of a choice," Will answered. "How do I get the loan?"

"Think about it for a while, and if you're sure you want to go through with it, give me a call at this number," he said, writing on a book of matches, "Randy Harrigian, Electronics."

"Why do you spell it 'Harrigian' instead of 'Harrigan?'" Will wanted to know. "Why the second 'I'? How do you pronounce it?"

"Four syllables, Hair-ig'-ee-un. It's part of being family. At least that's what my father-in-law says. His name is Muzafer Harrigian, his daughter's is Josephine Harrigian, and now mine is Randy Harrigian. Putting the 'I' in my name was one of the conditions of marrying Jo."

"Gus (that's Muzafer's nickname) didn't want his name to die out, and it sure as hell won't now, with four sons and another on the way. By the way," he added, "nothing like this will happen to you because you are just about the only friend I have but take a look at a few pictures in my wallet, as long as I have it out. Here are some snapshots of people who forgot to pay back money they had borrowed from AAAA Ltd."

The snapshots sickened Will. In color each victim looked like a survivor of a horrible catastrophe. Mangled and bloody faces here, ripped off ears there, fingers missing on both hands. He flicked the stack of photos back across the table with his middle finger, sort of holding it straight up erectly as a follow-through.

"Forget it," he said.

"Just kidding," said Randy, "AAAA Ltd is not that primitive. My father-in-law just gave me these pictures to show his clients in Fargo. I didn't ask where he got them. We don't ask each other any questions, but he trusts me. I served two years in Joliet rather than to say where some hot money I was carrying came from. Gus never forgot it, and after I got out, he summoned me to his home in Chicago. It was there that I met Josephine. He's really a great guy."

"You went to prison for him? Wasn't it rough there?"

"Joliet is not easy time, I'll tell you that. The only good part at all was when we put on our prison Christmas pageant. I did the makeup both years I was there. Aside from that, we always wished we could serve time in an Iowa penitentiary, where all they do is make license plates, and if their behavior is good, they get to make the ones that have short county names on them, like Ida, Lee and Sac. If they are a bunch of hard asses, then they get stuck with Appanoose, Poweshiek, Chickasaw, Allamakee, Pottawattamie, plates that take a hell of a long time to engrave."

"You're kidding again," Will chuckled. But maybe he wasn't. You never knew about Randy. There was that last game when they were seniors, going into the Mt. Vernon game undefeated. Randy was blocking back, Chad was quarterback and Will was a halfback. The day before the Mt. Vernon game at practice, Chad was clowning around calling signals in a real cocky way, "Hey diddle, diddle, right through the middle," "Wormy, wormy, oh so squirmy, here comes a long pass, right to Wormy," Will resented it, besides thinking it was piss poor poetry. But then, looking at Randy, Chad barked, "Dick, Dick, with the red headed prick, we want a touchdown, really quick."

Randy's philosophy had always been, "Don't get mad, get even," so the next evening against Mt. Vernon, he got three linemen to step aside at each pass play called by Chad, and the overgrown Mt. Vernon bruisers had Chad looking a bit like Randy's photos of clients who did not repay AAAA, Ltd. He was sacked 12 times in the first half, and although a sign in the locker room read, "There is a difference between pain and injury," Chad was taken to a hospital in Cedar Rapids where he stayed for at least a week. He never again called Randy, "Dick."

Will heard a loud movement of chairs through the partition, "My God, they're leaving already. Let's get back and see why," he said.

Randy looked at his watch, "Damn, I forgot to call home. The kids will all be in bed by 9:30, except for my oldest. Wolfgang is 11 now and stays up as late as he wants to. He's really into Nintendo games, but they are OK. It's after 9:00 now. I've got to get back to the motel and make that call. I've never missed one in all the years Jo and I have been married. Let me pay the tab and you try to cover for me at the rest of the reunion. I'm leaving for Tama at 6 in the morning. And I'll talk to the old man about that loan."

Back in the reunion room everyone was gone except for the five at the head table, Kathy and Missy, along with Smitherman and the aide from the rest home. Smitherman, head bowed low, had a small plaque balanced atop his bony wrists.

"Shame on you, you missed the presentation," scolded Kathy. "Where's Randy?"

"Had to leave. Emergency," Will said. "What presentation?"

"Professor Hupfer from the Education Department was here and gave Mr. Smitherman a plaque. They say he invented cooperative education by the Tea and Sympathy assignment he gave that day when we were seniors. At least a dozen students majoring in school administration have footnoted Mr. Smitherman in their doctoral dissertations." Kathy proudly pointed to the wheelchair. "This year alone they granted five more Doctor of Education degrees in their department. All working in cooperative education. Isn't that nice?"

"Yah, I'm really sorry I missed it," Will answered, "but why did everyone else leave?"

"To get to City Park in time for the fireworks. Three or four of them took chairs from the Athletic Club with them. We could be in deep trouble if they don't bring them back."

From the wheelchair, Smitherman raised his head an inch and mumbled, "They won't," and promptly went back to sleep.

"When you live in Chicago, you don't need special days for fireworks," joked Will, thinking of Randy, his father-in-law and AAAA, Ltd. "We have them every day there."

"Chicago," blurted out Smitherman, fully awake, "I'm going to Chicago next week. World War II navy reunion. You live there, Will?"

"Yes, sir," he answered, "here's my card. Stop in and see me if you have time." As soon as Will said that he felt silly, because he couldn't believe Smitherman could ever make it to Chicago in the first place. In fact, the old guy might not make it through the night. Smitherman was asleep again.

"Will I see you at the lake tomorrow?" Missy asked Will.

"Fraid not, too busy." Will turned to the wheelchair, "Well, I know you're asleep, Mr. Smitherman, but in case I don't see you again, congratulations on your award. And be sure to stop and see me in Chicago."

And to the man from the rest home, "Thanks for bringing him."

He headed out the door and checked in at the motel. "Maybe it wasn't much of a reunion," he thought, "but if I get out of debt, it's worth it."

Chapter 2

THE EMPTY HOUSE

Before returning to Chicago the next day, Will decided to take a look at his childhood home, purchased by his parents for $18,000 shortly after World War II. Viewing the house from the street, Will suffered pangs of loneliness, for the house (which he and Karen had sold after his mother got killed), for his happy childhood memories, but especially for his father and mother, both of whom died far too early.

It began with the death of Will's father of a heart attack when Will was in graduate school at the University of Chicago. Will could only attribute his father's death to parking meters, because the experience that triggered the heart attack was almost unbelievable.

The way his mother had explained it to him, his father bought ten minutes of time in the parking meter in front of the post office (the maximum time available), after which he carried Will's big birthday package to the end of the line at the post office windows. His mother said he just picked the wrong time of day to go to the post office, because usually more than one post office window was open. But for Will's father it was a day of bad luck. He no sooner worked his way to the middle of the line and his ten-minute parking time was used up, forcing him to take a chance on a parking ticket by staying in line, or running out to feed the meter, thus losing his place.

Also, because both parents loved Will very much, his father was not about to set the package down to be stolen when he returned to the car, so he carried it back and forth with him, into the wind, across the icy side walk, to the offended parking meter. Witnesses told Will's mother that on his father's third trip with the package he had a heart attack, dying instantly.

Add to that the humiliation to his mother, who when hearing about it three hours later, took a bus to the post office to pick up the car, and found that it had been towed away because of a meter violation. The whole series of events had made Will as angry as he had ever been in his life, but he buried his anger to comfort his widowed mother.

His mother's death was another miserable quirk of fate, occurring in California just four years after the death of her husband. She had finally resolved herself to her status and joined a newly formed widows' club in the community. What should have been one of the best times in her life, as the widows' club tour bus visited California on the way to a Bowl Game between the Hawkeyes and San Diego, turned out to be another horrifying event, as she was gunned down by a sniper's bullet while riding the tour bus on a freeway just outside of Los Angeles.

Mostly what Will remembered about her death was the TV newscaster who happily announced, "Fortunately, no others were killed or injured, and the Hawks ironically won their game." Will had wondered what was ironical about the game.

Will had no problems getting rid of the house after his mother died, selling it directly to a real estate agent for $75,000. What Will never found out was that the agent resold it the next month for $122,000.

As soon as Will got back to Chicago, he returned his car, stopped for a few drinks in a neighborhood bar and took a cab home. It was after nine, later than he had intended to return and beginning to get dark. As he fumbled for his keys, he wondered why Karen hadn't left on the hall light before she left for Memphis. After all, though they seldom traveled together anymore, they had followed sort of an agreement that the last one to leave the house would leave the hall light on. And she was still home when he had left town for the reunion.

From long habit he opened the front door and flicked the light switch at the same time. Nothing happened. Not plugged in, he thought. Picking up the remote-control switch, he clicked to turn on the TV, but again, nothing.

Something sure as hell was wrong here, he told himself. No lights, no TV and I can't even see. He remembered that Randy had written his name on a book of matches, so finding the matches, he lit one and headed for the phone to see if Karen had left a message on the answering machine. The phone was gone.

He went into his attached garage to his old '64 Volkswagen. It hadn't run for three months, but the lights might work. Flicking on the lights, nothing. He heard a knock on the front door.

Peeking through the window in the garage he saw a female silhouette pounding on the door. He stepped outside and from behind her, said, "You don't have to break down the door. Just ring the bell."

"Will, I've been ringing it for two minutes and nothing happened. It must not work. Why are you wandering around in the dark? Are you OK?"

It was Hildegarde, his dental assistant, whose husband was about as much fun to be around as Karen. Hilda had moved out a month before after running out of sufficient makeup to cover the bruises inflicted upon her nearly every Saturday night by her husband, Patrick O'Shea. He seldom beat her during the week, but that was because his job with the Illinois Highway Department usually kept him away from home from Sunday night to the next Saturday morning. And, as Hilda had said in defense of Patrick, he never beat her up unless he had first had at least two beers.

"Yah, I'm OK, except that someone disconnected the phone and cut off the lights and water over the weekend. Also, I don't know where Karen is. She should have been back this morning. How about you?"

"It's Patrick. Have you got time to come to the office?"

"Sure, I have nothing but time," Will said, getting into her car. "He hasn't been bothering you again, has he? Not that it's any of my business."

"Of course it's your business if your business is dentistry," she said pulling into the traffic. "It's a bit of a long story. Patrick called me up, nice as pie. All he wants is to have one of his front teeth fixed. Says my brother looked him up and beat the shit out of him for no reason. Asked if my family dental plan would still work for him even though we are going our own separate ways now."

Will remembered that in a flush of generosity, he had promised both his assistants and his receptionist free family dental care for as long as he stayed in the business. Patrick had been in only twice, having nearly perfect teeth, even better than Will's. Will had only two small fillings plus a smile that revealed an upper front tooth outlined in gold on the lower half.

"Where is he now?" Will wanted to know.

"He's right there by our office in the mall. Asked if I could get hold of you. I don't want anything to do with him anymore, but I don't want any trouble or a lawsuit," she said. "If you fix his damned tooth for free, then he can't sue my brother for the cost."

"What if the power is off in the office? Do you suppose Patrick will beat me up?" Will asked.

"Patrick never hits anyone except women," Hilda replied, "some kind of sexual hang-up. And the power is not off at the office. I pay the utility bills on time as fast as they come in. Our cash-on-hand is better than you might think. In fact, there is pretty close to a thousand dollars in the drawer right now."

"There won't be after I get there," said Will, as they pulled into the mall.

Chapter 3

THE OFFICE

By ten o'clock at night most of the mall shops were closed and darkened, but you could always be sure that Will's closest mall neighbor, the Christian Chiropractic Clinic would be all lit up and buzzing with patients until well after midnight.

Hilda parked right next to the three neon signs reading alternately, "Four Skilled Doctors," "Guaranteed Results," "Improve your Health for Jesus."

"He's over there," she said, pointing to a wooden bench in front of the Chiropractic Clinic. "I'll call you later," she added, dropping Will off. She sped away.

Recognizing Will, Patrick was bent over on the wooden bench, his jaw in both hands, looking very much like something he wasn't, namely Rodin's "The Thinker."

"OK, let's go inside," said Will, unlocking the door to the dental office and turning on the lights.

"It hurts, Doc, my God it hurts. Where the hell have you been?" Patrick asked, following Will into the office.

"That's not important," said Will, in his best professional voice. "What is important right now is to take a look at that tooth and get you out of pain. Let's go inside and take a look."

While examining Patrick's broken tooth, Will noticed that although the enamel was broken, thus exposing the dentin, the nerve itself was not exposed. Consequently, he knew Patrick's pain was somewhat psychological, since an exposed dentin is painful only when in contact with something cold, such as ice water, or more likely Patrick's favorite beverage, beer.

"The bad news," said Will, after examining the tooth, "is that your dentin is exposed, making it sensitive to anything cold, but the good news is that the nerve is still protected. We can take care of that right away."

"Well, then fix it, for Christ's sakes," demanded Patrick.

Will often worked without an assistant, especially at night with emergency jobs, and Hilda had acted as a dental assistant on a few occasions, but not tonight. She didn't even want to be within miles of any shopping center where Patrick might show up. You never knew when he would have two beers and start beating on her. Will knew she would call back in an hour or two after she was safely away.

"This will sting a bit," Will said after donning a pair of rubber gloves and preparing the local anesthetic. "Relax, and everything will be OK. I can fix that tooth so no one can ever tell the difference." Will was not one to boast, but he prided himself in his ability to match various shades of cosmetic bonding materials, right down to the last detail.

"UHHHH!" screamed Patrick, jumping halfway out of the chair, as the needle penetrated his gums above the fractured tooth.

"Sorry," said Will, knowing that with the dose of xylocaine he shot Patrick up with, the tooth would be numb within seconds.

"Why'd you have to numb my nose?" Patrick whined, "It's the front tooth that is broken. My God, can't you see the son of a bitch?"

"It will wear off in a couple of hours," Will answered. "Now let's get a perfect match for that broken tooth. We don't want it too white. We want it to look real."

"Perfect match, my ass," said Patrick. "I want the same thing you've got. Gold. If you dentists are rich enough to have gold teeth, why the hell shouldn't I have a gold one? Just because Hilda and I are washed up doesn't mean you can give me cheap dentistry."

Back in high school Will had broken the same exact tooth during wrestling practice one day after school when Chad deliberately smashed his elbow into Will's mouth. Will's mother had taken him to the dental school the next morning, and it was almost by accident that the gold tooth became part of his personality from that day on. It happened that the dental student working on Will on that particular day needed to fulfill two more gold requirements before graduation. Will hadn't really wanted gold, partly because his family couldn't afford it, but the dental student assured him that he would provide the gold at the same cost as a white filling. Years later, Will had considered having the tooth redone, but by then the gold filling had become part of his personality.

"If it's gold you want, gold you'll get," said Will, "but I've never been happy with mine. If you want gold, you will have to put up with some pain for another day and come back tomorrow. I'll take an impression today and mold your gold filling on my casting unit."

Will had kept his casting unit from dental school, although the only time he had used it was to make jewelry for Karen. In actuality he looked forward to using it again, this time for its original purpose.

"Come in tomorrow," said Will, "and we'll see what we can do."

"Whatever is the best," grunted Patrick, growing more civil by the moment as his mouth numbed. "You're paying for it, right Doc?" he sneered.

Will had good hands. The art teacher at SUI High had told him he would be a fine artist, with his attention to detail and his ability to shape the various elements of his pottery when they were doing their kiln unit, and later when they were on linoleum cuttings. The art teacher said he had never seen better, even at Pratt Institute in Brooklyn where he had done his undergraduate work.

Will had taken it as a compliment and thinking back on the incident gave him a great feeling of confidence, even when patching up the teeth of patients who had run their teeth clear through their cheeks in bike accidents or fist fights. At times he felt that dentistry was the only aspect of medicine remaining where the practitioner didn't turn everything over to a computer. Take dermatology, for example. In dental school Will had read that 99 44/00% of the diagnosis in that area was done by a computer. The dermatologist did the other 56/100 of one per cent.

After taking the impression of Patrick's broken tooth, Will said, "While I have you here, there are a few small cavities on your molars. Take me just a couple of minutes to fix them up. OK?"

Torn between suspicion and the joy of getting something for nothing, Patrick chose the latter, "Only a couple of minutes?"

"Yah, let's take care of them." Will inserted a different bit in his drill.

A few minutes later, the molars were patched with silver fillings, and Will said, "Don't bite on anything hard tonight. After tomorrow you will be as good as new. Let's take a look at my appointment book."

They walked together to main office, where Will looked at his next day's appointments.

"Can you come in tomorrow at three?" Will asked.

"Hell, I work all day. I go to work at eight and get off at five. Same hours as you're open."

"How about tomorrow night? Say, seven o'clock?"

"Nine is better for me."

"OK, nine." Will wrote in his appointment book in pencil - - - "Special - - nine o'clock."

As Patrick was leaving the office, Will said, "The numbness will wear off in two hours or so. If you have a problem, call." He gave Patrick his office number and said, "This is sort of a second home for me at times. Sleep right in the X-ray room. I'll hear the phone."

"Don't be surprised if you hear from me," Patrick complained, going out the door. Through the window Will watched him head for his pickup and pull out of the shopping center lot.

Will rather enjoyed working on Patrick's gold partial crown, and was pleased to note that his casting equipment had remained in working order, even during years of nonuse. What Will had no way of knowing, while working on Patrick's partial crown, was what lay in store for him in the days ahead.

The next few weeks were for Willard Mosley the most eventful of his life. How he survived them without going out of his mind was a question he would ponder for his remaining days.

He had once taken one of those cheap tests from one of those magazines favored by his two dental assistants. This particular test was headlined "Measure Your Stress . . . How Close Are You to the Funny Farm?" As he recalled, he had fared quite well on the test except that he was in debt. After all, he still had a wife, of sorts, a nice home, two cars, and a six-figure income. But had he taken the same test the day after he worked on his casting equipment, his stress score would have skyrocketed.

It began when Hilda came into the office at 9:00 a.m. and said "I just drove by your house, Will. They are having a sheriff's sale there for back taxes. Did you know about it?"

"Hell, no, I thought Karen had paid the taxes. I hadn't even looked at our checking account until I went to write a check to go to the class reunion. She must have been cleaning the account and salting away cash for a long time. They don't have a sheriff's sale for being just a day late on taxes. Not even in the Chicago area."

"Call over and . . ." Hilda started to say, before remembering that his home phone had been disconnected.

"The house is the least of my worries." Will thumbed through his wallet to see if he could get the names of anyone who accompanied Karen on the Elvis Presley Lives tour. "I don't even know where the hell Karen is. She ought to be back by now. It doesn't take more than an hour or two to go through the White House, so it seems like three days are plenty of time to see Graceland."

"What are you looking for?" Hilda wanted to know.

"Who went with her to Memphis. Maybe they would know."

"It's in the phone book. I saw it," Hilda remembered, "under EPL in the yellow pages."

"Look," said Will, "move all my appointments back two hours until I get back. I'm going to find out. May I use your car? Where did you say we had some loose cash for office expenses?"

"Here's the key," Hilda opened the fourth drawer on the right, uncovering a wad of "petty cash" and handing it to him.

"Whew," he whistled, counting the bills. "This is enough to run me at least a week if I keep it out of a checking account. Let's handle it this way for a while. As long as I'm living here there is no reason to deposit our receipts in the bank every day. Get them to pay cash if you can, and with the checks, run in and see if you can cash them at the Chiropractic Clinic next door. They do that lots of times for a fee."

With Hilda's car Will drove to the Elvis Presley Lives office, located just two blocks from Elmhurst College.

Opening the EPL office door, Will was greeted with an ear-shattering recording of "Jailhouse Rock." Strobe lights flitted through the area, landing on a middle-aged woman dressed in a cowboy outfit, standing behind four fake jail-cell bars.

"Hah," she spoke, "Ken ah hep you-all?"

"Yes," said Will, ignoring her accent. "My wife, Karen Mosley, took a tour bus to Memphis last week and I wondered if you knew where she was. Our house is closed and I'm afraid she is wandering around the whole Chicago area looking for me."

"So you ah Will," she said, "Well, you-all best not be lookin' in Chicago, cause she said she got herseff a job in Memphis and won't be back till she hits it big."

The news came as a genuine jolt for Will, but he was not completely surprised because of Karen's year or more of pocketing his property tax money, forcing their house up for auction the first time he was out of town. Someone who could do that could also decide to stay in Memphis without a word of explanation, Will decided.

"A job?" said Will, startled. "What kind of a job? Does she have a phone number?"

"Said sump'n about workin' right at the Presley Mansion and changin' her name. Had nothin' but bad luck with the name of Mosley. Said not to fret, cause it was nothin' pussonal about you. She pure and simple jist ain't comin' back."

"Shit," said Will, detesting the fake accent of the cowboy woman. He headed out the door.

Returning in Hilda's car to the mall, Will saw a small crowd gathered around his office gazing at what appeared from a distance to be the scene of a bicycle accident, with one body on the ground and a loose wheel rolling halfway between the dental office and the chiropractic clinic.

Hurrying to the scene, Will couldn't believe his eyes. On the ground lay Old Man Smitherman, blood oozing out of his head beneath his watch cap, the bulk of the wheelchair on top of him, backside up, bearing a bumper sticker reading "Don't Mess With Texas." No attendant was with him. Evidently he had wheeled his chair into the mall from a bus, wearing out the left wheel about three feet from the door.

"Hold everything," shouted Will at the gaping crowd. "I'm a doctor and he is my patient."

He lifted the wheelchair from Mr. Smitherman, turned his face up, breathing a big sigh of relief, as he noticed there was still life in his old SUI High teacher.

"Can you hear me?" asked Will, shouting into Smitherman's ear. "Are you OK? Don't move." Will ripped off part of his own shirt and dabbed around the blood, being careful not to hit a raw spot. The wounds appeared to be only superficial, except for the left side of Smitherman's nose, which was badly bruised, almost of the strawberry nature baseball players get when they slide into bases on a rough infield.

"I'm perfectly all right," answered Smitherman, with what appeared to be a completely lucid expression. "I can probably get up if you give me a pull. I don't really need a wheelchair, but I became so accustomed to it at the care center that I have been relying on it lately. Can you get someone to fix it, Will?"

"Let's see if you can stand up, if you are absolutely positive," said Will. Otherwise, I'll just lift you into the door and put you on my daybed until I get your wheelchair put back together."

As Will lifted Smitherman to his feet, two people from Channel Nine, at the shopping center for a package-tampering poisoning epidemic, asked Will for an interview.

"Can you wait till I get him inside?"

But it was too late. The camera was already zooming in on Smitherman, while the interviewer held the mike in Will's face, asking, "Who is this man? What happened?" while at the same time saying to her TV audience, "This is Ellie Plagger, live from the West End Shopping Mall, where a middle-aged man has apparently just rescued an elderly gentleman, after what appears to have been another shopping center mugging."

"How old is this gentleman," she asked Will.

As Will gritted his teeth, both in anger and from the exertion of lifting Smitherman into his arms to avoid tripping over the TV station cords, Smitherman himself answered, "I'm from out of town, a World War II Navy Enlistee, 85 years old. I rode in to get my teeth cleaned and the wheelchair broke. That's all. It is not really newsworthy."

"We'll give you a story," interrupted the portly assistant manager of the chiropractic clinic. "Hold the cameras right here. We're going to present this man with a brand-new wheelchair, and offer him a series of spinal adjustments, as we hope for a quick recovery. Call it public relations or whatever, but it happened right at our entrance and we are in the health business, today, tomorrow and forever."

Pushing out a new wheelchair for Smitherman was a gorgeous young lady wearing a nurse's uniform, complete with sheer white miniskirt revealing not only her calves, but also at least 80% of her thighs. The hem of her skirt was higher than the belt of the clinic's assistant manager, who patted her rump, while thanking her for the wheelchair.

While the camera was on the young lady and the new wheelchair, Will escaped through the front of his office into his crowded reception room, carrying Smitherman like a sack of flour and opening the door at the same time. Once inside he slammed the door saying to Hilda, "I'll be ready for the patients as soon as I bandage Mr. Smitherman's head and put him on the cot in the X-ray room. You can send in the first three now."

"Nice," said Smitherman, lying on the cot. Will gently washed around Smitherman's head and alongside his nose, sterilized the wounds and wrapped them neatly with two strips of white gauze. Then he covered him with a blanket, asked "How's that?" but got no answer. His old high school teacher had fallen asleep.

By going back and forth between two chairs at the same time and keeping the third chair free for emergencies, in the next three hours, Will handled 15 patients, a new record for him, but nowhere near the number of patients who went in and out of the chiropractic clinic in the same amount of time. Of course, they had three miniskirted nurses and four chiropractors, while he worked all alone, only occasionally calling on Hilda to assist during the more complicated root canal procedures.

After clearing up his backlog of patients, Will stepped into the X-ray room to see how Smitherman was coming. He had been lying on his back with his eyes wide open, studying the ceiling.

"Can I help you up, Mr. Smitherman?"

"I am quite capable of standing up," he replied, raising himself up by pushing his hands against the cot. "Do you have time to clean my teeth? That's partly why I'm here. They haven't been cleaned for five or six years." Smitherman was standing up now, brushing off his gabardine jacket and pulling out a pack of Chesterfields from the right inside pocket.

Will was astonished to see Mr. Smitherman turn all but the tip of the Chesterfield to a cylinder of ashes in four quick, deeply inhaled puffs. He had seen him perform this feat between classes at SUI High a few times but figured his lungs would be incapable of inhaling by now.

"I can fix this wheelchair in a minute, Mr. Smitherman. Let the clinic keep their new one. I left theirs outside, yours is here. It was just a publicity stunt on their part."

"I thought as much," Smitherman replied. "Wheelchairs are like shoes, blue jeans, gabardine suits and good wine. Not worth bothering with until they are at least a dozen years old. But I don't need a wheelchair, Will. The only reason I ever use it is the nursing home rules. All the males who seem to be too alert for their own good are stuck in wheelchairs and heavily sedated. It makes them easier to handle. Functionally equivalent to farmers putting rings in the noses of bulls and boars. They do it to all of us."

Pleasantly surprised at Smitherman's new-found ability to walk and to stay awake during conversations, Will led him to the first chair, and tilted it back, saying, "Now if you will lean back. And here, I'll get you an ashtray." Will bent over to rescue two cigarette butts Smitherman had ground into the floor and tossed them into the waste basket. After a brief search he came up with an ashtray.

With Hilda's assistance, Will gradually removed layer after layer of plaque and nicotine stains from Smitherman's remaining front teeth, all the while noticing that Smitherman was pleased with the idea of having Hilda working close by.

"You're in Chicago for a World War II reunion? How did you find us way out here?" Will asked.

Smitherman muttered and pushed Will's hand from his mouth, "Can't talk with my mouth covered up, Will. You ought to know that from the times we worked on vocal projection at SUI High. Reunion, yes, but it was rather a disappointment. Only 19 vets showed up from our old Destroyer Escort, and the ones that got here had aged a bit since the Great War, it was a lot of fun, but not the same as it was back in the 40's. They are beginning to lose the old zip that sent the

Japanese and Germans to their knees. Not to mention the Italians, but who counts them anyway? But I haven't lost mine. Now, to your second question, I rode a bus out here, boarded it somewhere in the Loop, got two transfers and plenty of help getting the wheelchair on and off all three buses. Then that last 100 yards where I was wheeling it by myself was a trifle rough on one of the wheels. Hope I didn't embarrass you any."

"Not at all. I'm fixing that wheelchair tonight and you are staying with me. Then I'll see that you get back home to Iowa. Don't worry about a thing."

"I'm not going back," said Smitherman, with a determined look on his face. "As long as I stay out of the state no one can order me back to the care center. I've checked on that."

"Why did you go there in the first place?" Will really knew from what his mother had told him, but he wanted to hear it for himself.

"It was rather irrational of them to put me away," said Smitherman. "They claimed I was senile. That was 12 years ago. Well, let me tell you something. Humans can grow out of lots of things, but they do not grow out of senility, and I am not senile now. I used to go into my old classroom at SUI high after they retired me, and they thought I had lost it because I was delivering lectures to an empty room, not counting the boxes of soap and cheap toilet tissue they stored in there. Do you think it's crazy to lecture when no one hears you?"

"No," responded Will, agreeably, but he had never heard of it.

"Well, I walked two miles every day to get there, meeting joggers who were running without going anywhere. Jogging was becoming fashionable at about that time. Also, I was passing other pedestrians who were walking just for the exercise. But what do they do? They lock me up because I was seeking a purpose from the exercise. What is the sense of walking somewhere if you don't do anything after you get there? The ones they should lock up are all those old bastards who walk in circles in the shopping malls every morning, just for the hell of it. Might as well be a bunch of gerbils on a treadmill as do that."

"I agree Mr. Smitherman, but why didn't you just walk there, look at the room, and turn around and walk back. Then no one would have complained. But to talk when no one is there. . . I've never studied law, but that was what they thought so unusual."

"Ever have the radio on and not listen? Do the announcers on Channel 9 become silent whenever you switch to Channel 2? Did you know that in the United States Senate during filibusters, we have our leading policy makers delivering lectures to empty chambers? Does the U.S. Army ever practice in peace time? Have you ever heard of a closed baseball, basketball, or football practice? Everyone performs at some time or other without an audience. But me? I do it and they lock me up. Piss on them. I'm not going back. Does that make sense to you Will? Is it logical to you, Henrietta?"

"It's Hilda," smiled Hilda, twitching his cheeks, "yes, it is very logical. And you don't ever need to go back. If Will can't keep you here, you can come stay with me."

Brightening up even more, Smitherman gave his best Groucho Marx leer and said, "You'll never be sorry about that decision."

It didn't take Will long to decide to let Smitherman live with him in the office. Hilda had been staying at a shelter for abused wives for two weeks and to Will's knowledge no males were allowed as live-ins at the shelter, not even if they were as harmless as Smitherman.

But about Smitherman. The contrast between his alertness here in the office and the way he had seemed to be pushing death at the reunion was little short of miraculous. Will had once watched a George Burns movie where three or four old men had discovered a swimming pool that acted as a virtual fountain of youth. But this was not the movies, it was real life. But at the same time, perhaps Smitherman was right, his sluggishness had been due to the pills they had forced down him for 12 years at the nursing home.

Also, Smitherman kept Will from feeling sorry for himself, and he was not bad company if he would quit grinding his cigarette butts into the floor. And Hilda? Well, with Karen gone and Patrick sitting on a court injunction to stay at least 100 yards away from Hilda, perhaps he and Hilda could learn to hit it off. He certainly had heard of good friendships blossoming into love, a much more likely result than passionate love growing into friendship. At least Karen could not really be classified as a friend the way she had turned out after the honeymoon.

Although there seemed to be no urgent need to repair Smitherman's wheelchair, Will enjoyed that kind of tinkering, so he straightened and tightened the spokes on the bad wheel. His dental tool kit could have been made for repairing spoked wheels, it seemed so easy. But by the time he had fixed the bad wheel it was so much better than the "good" one that he had to spend an equal amount of time on the "good" wheel to make the wheelchair ride evenly. After making a few final touches here and there, including smoothing and cleaning the "Don't Mess With Texas" bumper sticker on the back of the chair, you could say that Smitherman had wheels again.

Finished with his repair, Will looked up and asked, "Hilda, can you take most of the cash and go get both of us some new underwear and socks and a couple of shirts? We're both going to stay here tonight."

"Yes, sir," saluted Hilda. "Take me only 20 minutes. Your size must be about the same as Patrick's. That would be a 16 1/2 shirt. What length?"

"Short sleeves are good enough for July. Same for Mr. Smitherman. He must be a 14 collar by now. Used to be a lot more. And the underwear is really important. I'm going to get him to take a sponge bath when you are gone." Turning to Smitherman he asked, "What size underwear for you?"

They soon decided on regulation navy skivvies for Smitherman, which consisted of plain white T-Shirts size 38, and white boxer shorts, 36 waist, with stretch socks, medium, preferably navy blue. Will preferred sleeveless undershirts for himself, with boxer shorts, but with a 34 waist. He also settled on stretch socks, medium size, of any color. And almost as an afterthought, "Oh, and two hamburgers, a large order of French fries, and two cans of Pepsi. And get something for yourself, Hilda."

"I'll be back," she said, going out the door.

Smitherman was quiet when Will closed the office and said, "You clean up first in there," pointing to a sink beside Chair number 3. "I'll watch the door and get our clothes as soon as she brings them back. Then we'll eat something and call it a day. Aren't you tired?"

"Actually, no, this is the best time I have had for at least 20 years. When I'm not dosed with those drugs they hand out between bites at the care center, and when I'm not led to the toilet three times a day and once at night and when no one shouts at me, 'Have you had your BM yet today?' it all makes me so happy with life that I don't even think of being tired."

"How about the fall? The bump on your head, Mr. Smitherman? I wonder if we should see a doctor after you clean up." Will felt petty using the old trick "after you do this" to get Smitherman to cooperate, but it came out sort of automatically. He knew from his high school days that Smitherman thought modern Americans put too much emphasis on cleanliness, deodorants, cosmetics. The old man seemed to lump them all together, but it was encouraging that he had come in to get his teeth cleaned. Perhaps he could clean up all over to match.

"I'm certain the fall did not destroy my rationality," Smitherman said. "If we were to see a physician, he would most likely do exactly as you have done, wash and dress the wound and let nature do the healing. I don't heal as fast as I formerly did, but I have had injuries before and can distinguish between a serious one and the type that I have. And by the way, please stop calling me 'Mr. Smitherman,' the one thing I enjoyed at the care center was their addressing me by my first name. Call me 'Asa.'"

"We never knew you had a first name. You always signed just your last name on our papers, 'Smitherman.' OK, Asa, I won't feel really comfortable calling you that, but I'll sure give it a try."

"Did you ever wonder why I didn't put my initials on your papers after I checked them over? I'll tell you. My complete name is Asa Samuel Smitherman. Can you imagine what someone like that Chad fellow would have done with those initials? He seemed to have a nickname for everyone. As it was, the best he could do with me, and that was behind my back, was refer to me as 'that washed up fart.' But Will, I really do prefer 'Asa' to 'Mr. Smitherman.' Can you adjust to that?"

"I'll try, Asa. Now let's get washed up for supper. Hilda will be back soon."

After Hilda returned from her neighborhood shopping, Will set the new socks and underwear aside, pushed together two tables from the waiting room, pulled up three chairs and said, "Let's eat."

While they ate their hamburgers and French fries, Hilda noticed that Will was jotting things down on the French fry sack and asked him what he was writing.

"Making a list of things that have to be done in the next few days. I figure that we can decide right here after we eat, decide what we will do first, and then try to get a good night's rest."

"I'll help if I can," volunteered Asa. And possibly he could, thought Will, but he looked virtually helpless sitting there with his head and nose bandaged, watch cap on top of his head, white strands of hair hanging down on the sides and back.

"Do you always wear that cap?" asked Will.

"Every chance I get. I'm certain it cushioned my fall a bit when the wheel came off in front of here. They wanted me to wear a crash helmet in the care center, but after a few days when it caused abrasions on my head, they agreed to let me wear the navy watch cap. It is the only thing I have left from my navy career."

"I think it's cute," Hilda volunteered.

"Well, it looks as though we have a lot to do. Perhaps we can start tomorrow. Hilda, tomorrow morning I would like you to go to the law office two doors down and get the necessary forms so I can give you Power of Attorney. Then get all the cash you can muster up. . . How much is there, do you think?"

"After today, with some big insurance checks that came in, we have at least five thousand dollars."

"I have some cash on hand, also," said Asa. "About $85 and it is yours if you need it."

"Great, that gives us at least five thousand and eighty-five dollars, enough to make a big down payment on a used van. They have 'for sale' signs on half the vans parked in front of houses all the way from here to Chicago. Hilda, buy a van, use the money and get the van in your name. And see that it has a ramp so we can get the wheelchair in and out."

"Right, then what?"

"With the Power of Attorney, see what personal items are left in my house, or rather, what was my house before the sheriff's sale. Put what you think we really need in the van. Can you do all that by tomorrow night?"

"No problem. Then what?"

"How about closing shop for a few days and the three of us will drive to Memphis to see what really happened to Karen."

"Did you say all three of us, Willard?" asked Smitherman.

"Well, we aren't about to leave you here all by yourself and you said you were not going back to the care center. Are you up for the trip?"

"Absolutely."

That night in the dental office, Smitherman was asleep on the cot in the X-ray room before Patrick kept his appointment for his partial gold crown. Will was pleased to note that Patrick was neither talkative, nor inquisitive. He merely came and went, apparently pleased with his new gold tooth.

After Patrick left, Will stretched out on patients' chair #2. A real bed in his home would be more comfortable, to be sure, but Will had to face the fact that he no longer had a home. Neither, for all practical purposes did he have a wife, if she really had told the lady at the EPL club that she would not be back. But a lot of people think things like that, and most of them return. But he was not about to wait for her to return. They were going to Memphis, find out where she was, and talk her into coming home. They could get a new start. He wasn't even angry that she had practically stolen his hard-earned money to finance whatever she had in mind in Memphis.

The next morning, about a half hour after Will had risen from Chair #2 and had started a pot of coffee, Smitherman wheeled his chair into the reception room, saying "This works better than it did before they braked the left wheel at the care center a dozen years ago. You did a great job, but do you think I really need a wheelchair anymore? I can walk if there is always something to balance myself with. Perhaps a cane would do the trick."

"That's up to you, Asa." (Will still felt uncomfortable calling Mr. Smitherman by his first name, but practice would take care of that). "Why don't you use the wheelchair to exercise your arms, and whenever you go outside, we'll push you around just for the ride. I think you're doing fine."

"I'll use it. I especially appreciate the 'Don't Mess With Texas' sticker. Someone stuck it on the back of the wheelchair at the reunion, and I don't ever want to be without it."

"Well, for damn sure, if you don't use the wheelchair, you'll be without the bumper sticker, because that's the only one we have. I see them around here and there, but don't know what they mean or where to get them, except that it definitely has something to do with Texas."

"If Hilda could be with me when I'm outside riding in the chair, it will be quite tolerable, I assure you. But if anyone else pushes me around, I will either fall asleep or feign sleep. It is an old habit I picked up at the care center. When people think I am asleep they are less careful about what they say in front of me. That way I can tell what they really think of me.

"In the rest home whenever they thought I was awake they talked baby talk to me, 'eat your mashed potatoes, please, Asa, have another spoonful of blended carrots. Here, now let me help you. Here, be a good boy and take your medicine. Come on now, Asa, it's time for services. We'll have everybody's favorite hymns.' But when they thought I was asleep they said what they really meant to the other workers."

"Like what?"

"For starters, 'I wonder how long this old bastard is going to be around. He's at least 100 and if he died tomorrow no one could tell the difference. Look at the old goat. That silly black cap he wears. Someday I'm going to push him up to the top of the hill and give the wheelchair a shove out into the highway. That ought to wake up the old bastard.' . . . And Willard, that's one important reason I don't want to go back there, ever. I don't care if I die next week. Anywhere except that care center and I'll die happy."

Will was impressed with Mr. Smitherman's clarity of focus and vowed to himself that he could stay with him as long as he wished. Will once thought that the worst punishment one could mete out to an old man was to assign him to a teaching class at SUI high, but it seemed that in many ways, conditions at the care center were worse. Knowing Smitherman's fluency with the language, he was positive that at least once or twice Asa had proved that "care center" was another term to add to his list of misnomers, it was not the center of anything at all, and no one seemed to care about the welfare of the residents.

Hilda did not return from her van-hunting mission until the next morning, about the time Will and Asa were having their first cup of instant coffee. Looking well rested as she entered the door, she said, "Miracle of miracles. The van's outside, complete with hydraulic lift, air conditioning, cassette player, card table and refrigerator in the back, two cots and a convertible seat. We can get to Memphis and back without stopping for anything except gasoline and powdering our noses."

"All that for $5000?" asked Will. "How did you work that?"

"I'll never tell," said Hilda, seeing no need to explain to Will that she had added her own life savings toward the purchase of the van.

More interested in the "nose powdering" part of the conversation than in the purchase of the van, Smitherman said, "That's what the young ladies called it in the old days. . . 'powdering their noses.' We had a code word in the navy, too. We went to the 'head.' So if you two are sure you want me to ride along, I'll be careful to limit my nose powdering to any heads we may confront along the way. Unlike some of my less fortunates at the care center, I have never been troubled by incontinence. You won't have to stop every five miles for me, I can assure you."

Chapter 4

The Search

By 10:00 o'clock the next morning, Hilda and Will had everything packed in the van for the Memphis trip, had all appointments canceled for the next three days, and were just pushing Asa to the van when they saw Patrick lurking in the parking lot eyeing the three of them, but especially the van. Will thought little of it, but Hilda said, "He's been drinking again, I can tell. Let's get the hell out of here."

As they were pulling out of the lot, Will noticed Patrick shaking his fist at them from a distance, far enough from Hilda to comply with the court injunction.

"This is a first for me," said Asa, looking out the window from his wheelchair as they pulled onto Interstate 80. "Except for a short stretch of highway near Iowa City in the late 1960's, I have never been on an Interstate before. Since they put me in the rest home, I have been out of town twice for World War II reunions, and we took the Amtrak. Never the highway. It's an entirely new world out here on the highway."

"Well, enjoy yourself, Asa," said Hilda, cheering up with every mile separating her from Patrick, "you will like this ride better than the Amtrak. You can see in three directions at once from inside the van."

"If you get tired or need anything, just let me know," said Will from the front seat. "I'm going to lean back and close my eyes. You picked out a good van, Hilda, quite comfortable. This reclining seat nearly beats Chair #2 as a place to sleep."

Less than 20 minutes later, while Asa was reading the road signs aloud, he drummed up the closest he could come to a shout, "How fast have you been driving, Hilda? We have been on the road less than an hour and the sign says, 'Memphis 3 miles.' How can we be there so soon? I know I haven't been asleep, but we are there."

"No," Hilda said, "it means the road to Memphis is three miles. In fact, now it's two, then one. That means we turn south on I-55. Some road signs tell you how far it is to a particular town, and others let you know how far it is to the junction that takes you there."

"Confusing to say the least," Smitherman nodded off, his head dropping to his chest, looking almost exactly as he had at the SUI High Reunion, watch cap on his head, strands of white hair hanging down over both ears, completely at peace with the world, with only the bandages on his nose and the bump on his head indicating any difference.

But this time Will was not so certain Asa was asleep. Asa had told him he was off the rest home medication and that he was alert without the constant drugging, not to mention that Asa admitted having pretended to be asleep at the nursing home to enable him to hear what the attendants really thought of him.

Will took the bait, saying to Hilda, "Asa is a wonderful man, isn't he? Notices everything, excellent conversationalist, never complains. I think he is enjoying this trip, but I wonder if he knows why we are going to Memphis in the first place. I have never mentioned Karen to him, and naturally I did not mention that she is missing. Mr. Smitherman probably doesn't even know I am married."

"I know it now," Smitherman retorted, popping his head up from his clavicle. "You're right, I don't know why we are going to Memphis, but it is the best trip I have had since I took the troop train home from the war. You say your wife is missing? Perhaps I can utilize that bump on my head and conjure up where she can be located."

"What?"

"Dream of Karen. There are historical examples of people gaining precognitive powers after they injure their heads. I'd certainly like to help you find her, Will. At one time I rarely dreamed, but the last few nights I have had some vivid ones, but not about Carol."

"Karen," corrected Will.

"Of course. Did you notice that man who shook his fist at us this morning in the parking lot in front of your office? If it would help, I could try to dream about him too."

"My God," said Hilda. "He's talking about Patrick. Is it possible to dream of people you don't even know?"

"I don't know," answered Will, "I read about some man from Holland during World War II who got a bump on his head and acquired precognition, could foresee events before they happened. And it worked backward for him, too. He could touch someone's handkerchief or wallet and know where they were, or rather where the body was. And then there was that book by Stephen King, one of his first ones, I believe. Dead Zone. The main character in King's book could foresee the future after he had undergone some type of brain operation, as I recall. But of course, that was just fiction. You know Stephen King."

"Never heard of him," Asa responded. "In which period of literature did he appear? I'm astounded that I missed his works when I was teaching at SUI High. Ellery Queen, yes, but Stephen King, no."

"I get it," said Will. "King and Queen. Good one, Asa. But King wasn't writing until after you retired. That's why. But the important issue is, how is your head today? I'd rather have it heal properly than to exploit it for my own benefit."

"It's getting better. The only time I think it hurts is when you mention it, or you or Hilda puts on a new bandage. But bumps on the head could be irrelevant in dreams. Did I ever mention in class at SUI High that Samuel Clemens dreamed of his brother's death in May of 1858? In the dream his brother Henry was wearing Samuel's suit and in the casket he had a large bouquet of white roses with a single red one in the middle. Two weeks later his brother Henry died. Samuel went to the funeral home and the scene was exactly as he foresaw it in his dream, except for the lack of roses. Stretched out in a coffin he was wearing one of Samuel's suits. A moment later Samuel observed an older woman approaching the casket. She placed a large bouquet of white roses on Henry's chest. And a solitary red rose in the middle. And Samuel had dreamed all this without having had a bump on his head."

As they were discussing dreams and bumps on heads, Hilda was listening so intently that she had neglected to observe her speed on I-55, and the conversation was interrupted by the flashing red lights of a patrol car hailing Hilda to the shoulder. She braked the van, shut off the engine and fumbled through her purse for her driver's license. "Did you dream about any speed cops last night, Asa? Because you are about to see one. In fact, there are two."

The patrolmen stood, one at each front window, asked to see Hilda's license, one saying, "We've been clocking you since Joliet, Ma'am, and you have been over 75 miles per hour three different times. You can come sit in the car and see the radar reading if you wish."

"That's one I missed," said Asa from the wheelchair. "Wish I could do it

again."

"Do what?" responded the patrolman on the passenger side.

"Marquette and Joliet. I left that one out, also Lewis and Clark, Samson and Delilah, Abbot and Costello, Mutt and Jeff, and several more. That's what happens when you are in a hurry."

"What the hell are you talking about? You weren't even driving, Old Timer," said the holder of Hilda's license. "Why are you in a hurry? Are you going to the hospital? What's wrong with your head and nose? What happened?"

"Which question should I answer first?" asked Asa.

"Don't pay any attention to him, Officer," Will said, "He's living in the past."

"Well, you folks might not be living at all unless you hold down your speed. I'm giving you a citation, Ma'am."

"Citation?" asked Asa. "That's only the second time in my life I accompanied anyone who was granted a citation. That was in 1943 when we rescued some troops from the English Channel after their ship had been sunk by a German U-Boat. Citations were more difficult to earn in those days, although I will say that Hilda is a most excellent driver."

Ignoring Asa, the patrolman issued a summons to Hilda, told her she could pay the fine by money order or a certified check, and that if she failed to pay, the law would be upon her and assess a severe penalty. Finally, as he handed her the summons he cautioned, "Pay attention to the signs on this highway. It is clearly marked, and signs are posted there as reminders. When you see a posted sign on I-55, take my advice. Do what it says and you will be able to keep your driver's license for a long time."

Underway again, Asa was captivated by the highway signs, especially recalling the officer's warning to obey all traffic signs. "Hilda," he shouted," it says 'Exit' over there. You had best exit if the sign says 'Exit.'"

"He didn't mean that type of sign," said Hilda.

Will smiled, wondering what Asa would do if he drove by a sign that said "Clean Restrooms" or "Wet Pavement," literal translator that he was.

"How could this be?" Asa asked, seeing another sign.

"What?" Will wondered.

"It says, 'Watch for ice on bridge'. It seems highly implausible that ice would be on the bridge in the middle of July, but unless Hilda wants another one of those citations, she should stop the car, let me out, and I will wheel ahead and watch for the ice. I wonder how long I should watch?"

"You're funny," said Hilda. "What did you mean about Marquette and Joliet? I never went to college, but I've heard of them."

"It's a long story," said Will. "In high school he gave us an assignment to write about two individuals and we did the assignment with a partner. Randy Harrigan and I did ours on Leopold and Loeb. It was a long long time ago, but we made a big deal out of it at the reunion. What would you have done your paper on if you had been there?"

"Sonny and Cher."

"It was too long ago for them. But you could have picked 'Batman and Robin.'"

"If those road signs mean nothing," said Smitherman, "except for the speed signs, I'm going to rest my eyes for a few moments."

He really did fall asleep this time, waking up only as Hilda pulled into a large motel in the Graceland area of Memphis.

That night, after dinner and a few drinks at the motel, it was agreed that Will and Asa would share one handicap-accessible room, with Hilda in the next. All three slept well.

When Will awakened the next morning, he saw Asa sitting in his wheelchair, with Hilda rebandaging his nose and swabbing the bump on his head.

"It's looking better, Asa," said Hilda. "Travel must be good for you. In a week or so we can take those bandages off and throw them away."

"I don't mind the bandages one bit. You can change them every day for the next year if you want to. You have a much nicer touch than the people at the Care Center. They were a bit rougher on us than they needed to be. By the way, Will, if I'm going to be with you two in Memphis, I would like to help some if you can think of anything. Would you like me to go out for coffee? I could be back in no time."

"No, Hilda and I will be right back, but you could make a phone call or two for us if you really want to."

"Absolutely, but I haven't made five phone calls in the last dozen years. Whom shall I call and what should I say?"

"The Elvis Presley Graceland Tourist Center. Dial the main office and ask for the personnel manager. Ask if there is an employee named Karen Mosley."

"First I want to study this phone book. It is significantly larger than the one they have at the Care Center. I have always loved big books. But Will, I fear I will be unable to dial anyone from here." Asa had wheeled himself to the phone, the Memphis directory on the table directly in front of him.

"It isn't difficult to dial from here," Hilda said. "If you have a problem, dial 9 and the front desk will help you."

"There is no dial on this phone. How can one dial a number without a dial?"

"Oh," laughed Hilda, "It is called a dial, but it is easier than ever now. All you do is punch the buttons."

As she answered, Asa was looking at the page containing area codes, jotting down numbers on a pad provided by the motel management. "There certainly are more people in the world than I recall. To call the Care Center, which I am not about to do incidentally, under any circumstances, I apparently must punch in a 9, a 1, followed by a 319, and concluding with seven more numbers. That adds up to 913 billion, 193 million, 338 thousand, 128. How many phones are there back in Iowa? It is astounding."

"Here," said Hilda, somewhat confused by Asa's observation, "the number we want is local, right here in Memphis." Turning the pages, she located 'Elvis Presley Graceland Museum,' and told him to dial, (rather) punch those numbers, and offered to do it for him, but Asa insisted on doing it by himself.

With both Hilda and Will waiting in the room to see how the call went, Asa punched in a 9, a 1, and seven more numbers, making a mistake along the line and getting the front desk operator who asked, "What number are you dialing?"

"I'm not dialing," Asa responded, "just attempting to punch 913 million, 193 thousand, 429."

"Impossible," answered the operator, "what room are you calling from."

"This one," said Asa, overlooking the sentence-ending preposition, the best he could.

As he punched in a series of numbers once more, the operator still on the line, he was beginning to get somewhat frustrated, though he seemed to enjoy the process.

"Let me dial . . . punch," offered Hilda, "then ask for the personnel manager."

"And what will you ask him? "

"I honestly cannot remember," she said.

After thinking a moment, Asa answered, "Do you have a Karen Mosley in your employ?"

"Right." With one hand Hilda punched in the numbers, patting Asa on the arm with the other. "Here."

"We had better wait and see what happens," said Will quietly.

Getting an answer, Asa said, "I wish to speak to the Director of Personnel."

"May I ask who is calling?" was the response.

"Certainly, of course you may. I want the Director of Personnel."

"Excuse me, sir, may I ask who is calling?"

"I believe I have already responded to that query in the affirmative. Indeed you may ask. As a matter of fact, you have done so twice by my count. I want the Director of Personnel."

The operator hung up, leaving Asa nothing to hear but the dial tone.

The three had breakfast in the motel restaurant, after which they returned to the room briefly, called the front desk and ascertained that checkout time was noon. Will figured they could find Karen, get her things, check out of the motel at noon and be on their way to Chicago by one p.m. But he was uncertain, recalling the lady in the Elvis Presley Lives Club office in Elmhurst, who had told him Karen would not be coming back.

With time a genuine priority, however, he decided to check out before going to the Presley Museum, and it turned out to be a good move, because they were destined to spend most of the day amidst the hordes of tourists and a few cultists at the museum.

It was but a brief drive down Elvis Presley Boulevard to the museum, a large plane, owned by Elvis, clearly marking the museum area. They pulled into the parking lot, already three-fourths filled at 9:30 in the morning, got out of the van, together with Asa, and started the trek across the newly blacktopped parking lot to the museum center.

While being pushed in his wheelchair, Asa had historically dropped his head onto his chest, feigning sleep, but the Presley parking lot was so stimulating to him that he kept whipping his head from left to right as Hilda pushed him between rows of parked autos, vans, pickups, campers, a few semis, and a bus or two. What stimulated Asa were the bumper stickers.

As he passed between two rows of vehicles, he seemed a bit like a tour guide as he audibly read the bumper stickers, "Support your Local Police," "National Rifle Association," "Thank God, I'm American," "Jesus Saves," "WLS, Nashville," "Grand Old Opry," and finally he shouted to Hilda, "Stop, please."

"Are you all right?" she asked.

"Here's one exactly like mine. 'DON'T MESS WITH TEXAS,'" he said. "How do I get some more of these?"

"They might sell them here at the Visitor's Center," Will answered. "If they don't, it is the only thing they are missing."

"Someone stuck that 'DON'T MESS WITH TEXAS' sign on my wheelchair at the SUI High Reunion. I had my eyes closed at the time to listen more carefully, but I cannot remember who put it there or where it was originally obtained. I could use a few more of those signs. I wonder what it means, 'Don't mess with Texas.'"

"We will find some," said Will. "All you want."

Just inside the Visitors Center, Will asked Hilda to stay with Asa near the door, where a large ashtray was visible for the use of smokers. Judging by the "Thank You for Not Smoking" sign, smokers were supposed to snuff out their cigarettes in the tray before entering the ticket office and souvenir shop.

As Asa crushed out his cigarette in the ashtray, he asked Hilda why people displayed "Thank You for Not Smoking" signs when someone was smoking. "Isn't that a bit analogous to saying, 'Thank you for not bumping into me,' right after the very person has run over you?" asked Asa.

"Probably," said Hilda, "Will you be OK for a minute or two while I go to the rest room?"

"Certainly," said Asa, lighting up another Chesterfield.

Will was having no luck at all at the ticket office or anywhere else in the Visitors Center locating his wife. No one had ever heard of Karen Mosley, though a secretary did have a record of the Elmhurst Chapter of the Elvis Presley Lives Club having attended on July 4 and leaving on the 5th.

Just as Will and Hilda were approaching Asa from different directions, a man with a toothsome grin, a pastoral collar and cowboy boots stopped in front of Asa, pointed his finger at him, saying, "Those cigarettes are the work of the Devil. Hear Ye, Hear Ye, the Lord wants ye to cast it away."

"I am the only one here," said Asa, looking around, as Will and Hilda listened in to the conversation from a distance.

"My point, exactly. Cast away your cigarette and make way for the Lord," repeated the preacher.

"From my early studies of English grammar, I learned that 'Ye' is plural. There is only one of me. Definitely singular," said Asa. "Do you work here, Father?"

"Don't call me Father. Here, have my card," the preacher offered, handing one to Asa, who read "Reverend Billy Bob Barker, Seismic Churches of America."

"Thank you," said Asa, reading the card and snuffing his cigarette into the ashtray.

Hilda and Will chose to ignore Reverend Billy Bob Barker, and as they reached Asa, Hilda asked if he was all right.

"All except for a headache, never had any really bad ones in my life, but as soon as I saw this preacher person up close, and as soon as he opened his mouth, my head began to throb. Felt it right beneath the bump you rebandage each day, for which I thank you."

Worried about after-effects of the bump on Asa's head, Will asked if this was the first headache he had experienced since the accident in the shopping center parking lot. Asa responded that he had suffered only two headaches, one with Reverend Billy Bob Barker, and the other the previous morning when that man (who turned out to be Patrick) had shaken his fist at their van. Will did not pursue the point, but said, "Let me know if it gets worse."

Will changed the subject and asked Hilda and Asa if they wanted to visit either Elvis Presley's plane or the mansion while they were there.

"Just about everyone visits the mansion," Will said.

"I'm game for it," Hilda said, "the way people talk, there is something very spooky about that mansion. There is one part of it they do not allow the public to visit. Two ladies in the restroom said they had visited the mansion six times each, or was it seven? At any rate, in all cases, the stairs leading to the upper bedrooms are roped off and no one is allowed to go up there."

"I'll buy the tickets," said Asa, "the only other thing I need money for is Chesterfields, and I have two cartons in my luggage, enough to last me for at least a week."

"No, this is on me," said Hilda, going to the ticket office.

Tickets in hand, Hilda followed approximately 50 tourists out of the building to the curb, where a bus was due any moment to take them to the mansion. In fact, before Will, Asa, and the wheelchair had caught up with the group, three identical small buses pulled up alongside the curb, each unloading a group of passengers coming back from the mansion.

"My God, there she is," said Will, indicating the inside of the first bus. Karen Mosley was the driver, telling the passengers, "Step down carefully, please, now on this side you will see Elvis's little old plane, and around the corner here are some little old souvenir shops, a little old cafe and some movies you can watch on the life of Elvis. Thank you all for visiting Graceland, come back now, you hear?"

She recited the entire spiel in a southern accent, somewhere between that of Dollie Parton and Lady Bird Johnson. Fantastic, Will thought. She had been here less than a week and had already acquired a southern drawl. He had a slight problem accepting her new Dixie accent. However, Karen had always adopted regional speech wherever she visited, if only for a weekend. Once after her club met two days in Duluth to visit the home of a former rock star, she came home talking like a Finnish immigrant.

"Good Lord," Will smiled to himself, listening to her parting words to the passengers, "if she were a pet dachshund and spent a week in Mexico, she would come home barking like a Chihuahua." But the dog with Karen on the bus was not a dachshund, he noticed. Behind her as she was standing, Will could see a small poodle curled up in the driver's seat.

As soon as Karen's passengers were unloaded, she took a spot behind a rope gate of sorts in front of the passenger entry to the bus and awaited the next tour. It was then that Will's eyes met Karen's and before he could get in a word, she announced quietly, "I'm not going back, Will. It's all over. For the first time in my life, as Reverend Billy Bob Barker told me, I have found a purpose. Will, I have been reborn. I am a child of God and will continue to be until the end of time."

Will probably did not want to admit it, even to himself, but what had begun with a search for Karen with the hope of getting her to return home, had in all actuality resulted in an effort on his part to close the door on her part of his life. If he could get some of the house money back that she had pocketed for her Memphis trip instead of paying the bills and taxes, he would consider himself fortunate.

"Karen, I saw this coming a long time ago. Why we remained married as long as we have is a mystery to me also. All I want is some money. Whatever you took from the house money for the past several months is probably enough to keep me and my office afloat for a few more weeks. The house was sold for taxes. I have no credit at all. Just a small amount of cash. Whatever you have, I'll be happy to settle for half. Does that sound fair?"

He surprised himself with the rational way he looked at their lives and the "solution." After all, she had deceived him by spending money that was not really hers to spend. A lot of men would be quite angry, he knew. But all he wanted was to write it off. To him Karen was a Chapter 11 bankruptcy case, and he would be more than happy to settle for 20¢ on the dollar.

"My name is not Karen any longer. It is Deborah. And I have no more money. I divested myself for the honor and glory of Jesus, and Reverend Billy Bob Barker is helping me to lead a better life after my divestiture You cannot be divested of your sins, Reverend Billy Bob says, unless you first divest yourself of your money. He also has my Power of Attorney, incidentally. Look, I have just two minutes to load this van and take more guests to the mansion. There is no reason to talk about it. Nothing will change. I have made up my mind and have found Jesus. Besides that, you are upsetting my poodle, which is a gift from Reverend Billy Bob. Please go back. I am filing for divorce, making no demands because you have absolutely nothing except a string of debts."

The bus passengers had already begun to give up on riding Karen's bus and were making a beeline for the next two buses. Will wondered how many buses there were here at Graceland.

"Anyone bothering you, Deborah?" queried a voice from the rear. Will turned and noticed the clergy collar and knew immediately that he was viewing The Reverend Billy Bob Baker. Smitherman's head had slumped down to his chest and he appeared to be in pain as The Reverend approached.

"No, Reverend," explained Deborah (nee Karen), "it's just my ex I was telling you about the other evening. He's OK."

"Well, if he's OK or not OK, the question is, are you going to take your break? I thought this would be break time for you, so I've been waiting."

"Oh, goodness, it is break time. I plumb forgot."

Will had so many things running through his mind it was hard for him to concentrate. First his wife insisted she was Deborah, not Karen. Next, the preacher fellow seemed to have some type of interest in her (which was all right with Will). But third and most important, what did the preacher and Patrick have in common that would cause Smitherman to get headaches? Now Will was getting one. He wanted Smitherman to tell Billy Bob Barker that "Reverend" as a title is an adjective, not a noun, consequently it should be preceded by "The."

Perhaps the reverend was a phony one, or else the clergy was accepting illiterates these days. If Asa were only awake he could probably explain.

"Here's my card, Sir," said Billy Bob. "At your service, Seismic Churches of America."

"How long a break do you have, Karen?" Will wanted to know.

"My name is Deborah. Anyone reborn is born with a Biblical name. Billy Bob said so."

"Is Billy Bob a Biblical name?" asked Will.

"It's his preacher nickname. All southern preachers have nicknames. His real name is Babylon, but they call him Billy Bob," she explained.

"Has your pet poodle been reborn?" Hilda asked scornfully. Will caught her eye and shook his head slightly, not wanting to create a scene.

"As a matter of fact, yes my poodle has been reborn. Who the Hell are you? Oh, I get it," Karen snapped, "You're Will's so-called assistant. It certainly didn't take long for you to hop in bed with my husband the first time I turned my back, did it?"

"Look, let's forget the whole thing," said Will. "If it makes any difference nobody has hopped into bed with anybody unless you and Billy Bob got acquainted fast. On second thought, maybe that is what you meant by divestiture. I'll bet you divested more than my money to this quack."

With the Reverend Billy Bob Barker taking it all in, ready to intercede if it suited his interest, Karen said in a newly hushed voice, "Billy Bob saved this entire area from an earthquake in December of 1990. Just a few miles from here, over in Missouri, the whole earth was about to open up, and Billy Bob led his members of the Seismic Church in prayer and stopped it. And Will, it won't be so easy for him to stop it next time unless people start being a bit more appreciative. Right, Reverend?"

"If enough people keep divesting, I can hold off an earthquake," said Billy Bob, modestly. "But the ways of the Lord are not to be taken lightly."

"And the only good thing that will come of the quake when Billy Bob can hold it back no longer is that when it happens, the stairs in the

Graceland mansion will crumble and all of us will be able to go up and talk with Elvis. He's up there, you know."

"Well, I'll tell you one thing," Hilda volunteered, "we're not about to visit that mansion. So, when you brag to the tourists with that bullshit about 600,000 people visiting the mansion this year, you had better correct yourself and make it 599, 997. Because none of us are going," pointing to Smitherman, who was feigning sleep in the wheelchair.

"I'll visit it on one condition," said Smitherman, suddenly alert, "if they give souvenirs and if they have the one for which I am looking."

"What's that one, Old Timer," asked Billy Bob.

"I want two or three more bumper stickers that say, 'DON'T MESS WITH TEXAS.'"

"I can sell you one that says 'Jesus Saves.' That will do you more good if you seek Heaven than 'DON'T MESS WITH TEXAS.'"

"Well, I could get a 'Jesus Saves' sticker and add a word or phrase. All good bumper stickers that I have ever seen have objects. For example, 'Jesus Saves String,' or 'Jesus Saves S & H Green Stamps or coupons,' or something on that order. But I really love those 'DON'T MESS WITH TEXAS' stickers. In the great war I was a radio operator and everything we typed was in capital letters. There was no lower case, you see. And these 'DON'T MESS WITH TEXAS' stickers remind me of that. The Texas bumper stickers have captured my imagination, you might say."

"You have made that very clear." said Hilda with a smile, and turning to Karen, she said, "One question before we leave, Karen."

"It's Deborah."

"When your poodle was reborn, did it take on a Biblical name?"

"I'll answer that," said Reverend Billy Bob. "Indeed, we had some problems. Dogs are mentioned only a few times in the Good Book, but in the Book of Revelation we found a reference to a dog named Moreover. Moreover is a Biblical name for a dog and our little poodle bears that name."

The poodle uncurled itself from the driver's seat, hearing the name "Moreover" two times.

"I happen to know the Bible," announced Asa skeptically from his wheelchair. Exactly what does it say about a dog named Moreover? Do you mean Rover? That is not in the Bible."

"I can clue you in on the Moreover documentation right now. I can quote it Chapter and Verse," said Billy Bob. "In Revelations we read of the awe-inspiring events taking place near the end of time."

"The Missouri Earthquake, for instance," said Karen.

Billy Bob continued, "The Book of Revelations speaks of devastation and in simple black and white says, 'Moreover, the Dog howled at the moon.' If that doesn't tell you Moreover is a Biblical name for a dog, I don't know what further evidence you need. Unless, as your ex-wife seems to indicate, you are a victim of Secular Humanism."

"I certainly don't need to hear any more of that happy horse shit from either of you," said Hilda, getting ready to leave.

"Nor, I," Smitherman added.

"Good luck to both of you," said Will ignoring the Secular Humanism crack. "When are you filing, Karen?"

"It's Deborah. I have already filed. You will get the papers when you get back to Chicago. But as long as you're in Memphis, you really should see Graceland. Elvis bought it in 1956 for $100,000 and during the time he lived there he found Jesus and divested a lot of his wealth to the church. And I, for one believe he is still upstairs, waiting for the earthquake. Come on Billy Bob. Ride with me up the hill to bring some tourists back. The two of us can sing 'Hound Dog' when we get a load of passengers. Who knows, there might be a Hollywood scout here today."

Will, Hilda, and Asa returned to their van in the Elvis Presley Parking Lot, without conversation on the way, except for occasional comments by Asa on the variety of bumper stickers attached to the pickups, campers and RV's. Asa especially enjoyed "Spending Our Children's Inheritance" appearing on a huge Winnebago.

"Winnebagos are manufactured in Iowa," said Will to Asa, "But you know that."

"Yes, it's a new outfit, am I correct?"

"Relatively new, yes. I do not know of the exact year they started production in Forest City. I think I was just out of high school."

"Seems like yesterday, doesn't it?" acknowledged Asa, who thought anything less than 30 or 40 years old was new.

"What do you think of Elvis Presley?" inquired Hilda, as she pulled the wheelchair up to the van.

"I realize he is new, too, and that is the problem. I can't quite get accustomed to what they call 'Rock and Roll,' although two songs I heard in there seemed familiar, except that he changed the words, if that was indeed Elvis Presley."

"Which two?"

"'O Sole Mio' and another one I can't think of just now. I heard it during the war."

"He means, 'Love Me Tender,' I believe," Will volunteered. "The tune is from 'Laura Lee' or something like that."

All was quiet as they drove from the parking lot, until Asa picked up on the music conversation. It was clear that he had been thinking about it and wanted to continue. There had been little meaningful conversation during his years in the Care Center.

"Despite Shakespeare's admonition about a man who has no music in himself being fit for treason, stratagems and spoils, I personally detest most songs," Asa expounded. "They are illogical. But when they make a musical of a story, it is abominable. Back in my younger days, the department head gave us tickets to watch 'West Side Story.' I watched with the other faculty members, but for only a few minutes. We were all seated together according to departmental rank, with the dean in the center, two full professors on either side, balanced by three associates and two assistants. They had instructors sit on the edge, two graduate students and me. As it developed, two characters in the play had a fight and one knifed the other, killing him in a street fight. The killer, hurrying to the home of his girlfriend, who happened to be the sister of the slayed victim, jumped upon her balcony, as I recall, after which she approached, singing angrily, 'Tonight, tonight, you killed my brother tonight,' or words to that effect. Not to be vocally outdone by a female, the slayer joined her in perfect harmony. It was very unrealistic, the two singing together within moments after he had murdered her brother. I could not accept such incongruities and left the theater. It was shortly after that occasion that I was sent over to SUI High to finish my career."

"You are a sweetheart," said Hilda, "isn't he sweet, Will?"

"No question about that. Besides, it appears that with Karen (or is it Deborah) now out of my life, I have only three friends, but fortunately, all three are sweet."

"Who are they?"

"Well, there's Asa of course, and Randy . . ."

"And? . . ." Hilda waited.

"I must be getting old," teased Will. "The third escapes me at the moment."

They had not been driving long when they noticed a "New Madrid - - 10 Miles" sign on I-55. As usual, Asa was the first to notice it.

"Is that where that Seismic Billy Bob was telling us about?"

"Yes, they predicted a big earthquake there in 1990, December I believe, do you remember?" Will asked.

"I was not one to keep up with the news at the Care Center. I should keep track of events, but no one mentioned it there. But about the sign, is New Madrid really 10 miles from here or is the place we leave the highway to reach New Madrid ten miles from here? Which one, Hilda?"

"Great job, remembering," she said.

Asa frowned, "If you ever need a job, just keep talking like that and you will be qualified to boost morale at a nursing home. They always talked to us as though we were infants. And of course, none of us were."

"I'm sorry," said Hilda, sincerely, "It's a bad habit I picked up working with patients at Willard's office. It does seem true, though. Those of us in the area of health most always seem to address the patients as though they were small children. Certainly you are not a small child, Asa. You're a big boy, and damned good company too. But about the10 miles. It is ten miles to New Madrid and also ten miles until the New Madrid junction. Get it?"

"No, I do not," said Asa "but if you want to confuse me with numbers, try this. If three people are riding in a van and see a sign reading, 'New Madrid - - 10 miles,' how far is it for each of the three. How would you solve that problem, Hilda?"

As Hilda chuckled, Will said, "Now if you had asked Karen (or Deborah) that very question, she would have taken out paper and pencil and worked on it for a while. Unless since she has been reborn, she has also acquired a new mind."

"Don't be bitter, Will," Hilda chastened, "It is not like you, even though you have every right to be. Actually, I don't know which of us has (or had) the worse marriage, you or me."

"You or I," corrected Asa, "subject of 'had the worse marriage.'"

On that note, they arrived in New Madrid, found a motel, checked in, ate, and decided to visit one of the souvenir shops that had popped up during the 1990 Earthquake publicity. Noting Asa's liking for bumper stickers, they surveyed some that said, "EARTHQUAKE, MY FAULT," "I SURVIVED THE BIG ONE," and simply "NEW MADRID, 1990." Asa passed up on those, saying the one he truly liked was the one he already had.

"But if you see a new 'DON'T MESS WITH TEXAS' sticker, let me know," he said, wheeling away from the display of bumper stickers.

"How about a muscle shirt?" asked Hilda. "Here's one that says, 'Danger, I'm at Fault, New Madrid, Missouri, the Show Me State.' Would you like that, Asa?"

"You would have to be more muscular than I to wear a shirt with that many words visible to the onlooker," Asa responded.

"How about a big pin for your watch cap? Here are some Cubs pins. Do you follow the Cubs?"

"I certainly do. Believe it or not, I was too young to remember when they won the World Series, but I was alive then, which is more than you can say for at least 98% of the Cub fans in this country. It was in 1907 and 1908. They won the Series both years. Beat the Tigers handily. It is possible that I may live to see them win another. They came close in 1945, against the Tigers again, but have not made it to the Series since."

"Is this the first time you ever wore a pin on your cap?" Hilda wanted to know as she attached the Cubs pin to Asa's watch cap.

"In '36, when I was teaching in Kansas I wore a Landon and Knox pin. Landon and Knox," he said excitedly to Will. "We forgot that one, too."

"I guess so," agreed Will.

"Did Landon and Knox win many games?" asked Hilda innocently.

"No, they were worse than the Cubs, if that's possible."

Will was enjoying the conversation and hated to shut it off, but he finally said, "We've had sort of a trying day. Shall we go back to the motel and get some rest? We have a big week ahead in Chicago, and I want to get back on schedule within two or three days, if that's possible. If I go broke without the assistance of Karen, rather Deborah, I have only myself to blame."

"Don't worry about your work, Will. I have worked in three dental offices during my career, and you are by far the best of the lot. You have had a heavy cross to bear, considering your marriage, if you want to know what I think about it. At times the only thing that kept me going with Patrick was knowing that you got probably a worse deal from marriage than I did. If that's possible."

That night in the motel the three made the same sleeping arrangements as the night before, with Asa and Will in one room and Hilda in the other. Will had lifted the sleeping Asa from his wheelchair and plopped him gently atop one of the double beds, after which he removed his shoes, socks and trousers, leaving the watch cap on his head, for fear of awakening him.

"It's almost the same as having our own child, isn't it?" asked Hilda quietly.

"Almost, I guess, but I'll never know for certain because I've never had one."

"At times you sound more like Asa than Asa does," she said, laughingly.

Will seemed to take the remark as a compliment and asked Hilda, "Did you ever read Hemingway's For Whom the Bell Tolls?"

"Huh?"

"A novel we had to read in Mr. Smitherman's class in high school. Novels were not quite so frank when Hemingway wrote it during the Spanish Civil War just before World War II. But for the two main characters in the story, something happened whenever they had sex."

"What happened."

"The earth moved."

"My God, Will, I think I felt it move tonight. Twice in fact. And without sex. I can't believe it."

"I felt the earth move, too," said Will.

From the darkened room came the voice of Asa Smitherman. "I felt the earth move, also, and would venture that everyone not fast asleep in New Madrid experienced the same sensation. It was a small earthquake. Not enough to cause any damage, but just enough to make the experience memorable. Once when I was ashore in Sicily in World War II there was a severe earthquake. But this one tonight and the one they had in Spain for Hemingway's characters were practically nothing."

"Asa, go back to sleep, or I will put a dirty bandage on your head tomorrow and take away your Chicago Cubs pin," Hilda threatened.

"I might be 85, but I am not too old to take a hint. For the remainder of our stay in New Madrid, I can assure you, it will be all quiet on the Western front."

Chapter 5

THE CODE

After breakfast the next morning the three followed I-55 North for the remainder of the trip, Hilda holding the speed down, Will, next to her, offering to help with the driving at any time, and Asa in his wheelchair in the back of the van reading highway signs. Noting one he had not seen on the trip down, he said jokingly, "That explains why that one lad went to Canada."

"What lad?" asked Will.

"That chap on the football team with you. Chad, as I recall. He went to Canada. I never did understand why until I saw that highway sign just now."

"Which sign was that?"

"The one that beckons us to 'Drink Canada Dry.'"

"Ugh," Hilda moaned, "but that's a good one, Asa. Any headaches last night?"

"None."

"Any dreams?" Will wanted to know.

"None that I can remember."

Returning to the suburban shopping center west of Chicago, Will unlocked the door, and was about to open for business, catching a few walk-ins toward day's end, but before he and Hilda could get organized the phone rang.

"Mosley's Dental Clinic," said Hilda. . . . Will? yes indeed, he is right here."

Will picked up the phone. It was Randy at the other end of the line.

"Where in hell have you been," Randy asked. "I've been trying to get hold of you for two days. No one answers at your house. And no one at your office. Can we talk?"

"As far as this end is concerned, yes, if you mean wiretaps. The only people who have reason to tap my phone are the IRS and they don't need to tap the phone in order to hang me. I've got about 30 more days to settle out of court with them. Otherwise, I'll be making license plates too."

"Will you be at the office for a while?"

"We just got back, sure."

"No, I have a better idea. Let's eat together tonight."

"I'd ask you to my house, but I don't have one anymore."

"Can you be at O'Hare in an hour?"

"Sure. Where at O'Hare?"

"I'm in a phone booth next to Ozark lines. You'd better hurry before they go bankrupt and change the sign. Airlines do that a lot these days."

Leaving Hilda with Asa at the dental office, Will took a cab to O'Hare, found the Ozark window and was looking for the phone booth when Randy tapped him on the shoulder.

"Let's walk," said Randy. "Can you walk and talk at the same time?"

"That's a hell of a question to ask your former high school teammate."

"Well, let's start." As they walked through O'Hare's corridors, Randy explained to him that he thought he could get him a sufficient loan to enable him to pay off the IRS, and if Randy was interested he could work as an adjunct dentist for AAAA, Inc.

"You mean be the group dentist for AAAA? Why would they want to hire me as a dentist?"

"It's part of that multicultural, non-sexist stuff. AAAA is trying to be the first corporation in America to add 'multiprofessional' to its brochure. A dentist will help. Don't worry about it, though. We already have an actor or two in AAAA. Why not a dentist?"

"Is it an actor I might have heard of? " Asked Will.

"You're looking at him," answered Randy. "Or to be more exact, I do a lot of backstage work in community theater. AAAA acquired an old opera house on the south side of Chicago, and I help out a lot."

"Doing what?" asked Will.

"I do makeup. They say I'm pretty good, if you don't mind my sounding a bit more than humble. Or should that be 'a bit less?' Made up a teenager the other night and she could have passed for 75. Except for her voice, that is, but the best makeup artists in the world can't do a thing about that."

"OK," Will acknowledged. "But about the dentist part. Where would my office be? The office is about the only stability I have in my life, now that I have lost my house, my car, my furniture and my wife."

"Lost your wife? She died?"

"Left me, but I don't really care. Saw it coming a year or two ago. It had to happen."

"Keep your office. AAAA will come to you, but we can't talk on the phone about it. We are having a few problems that must be resolved right now. You will be reading about it in the papers tomorrow if you haven't heard already."

"You make it all sound so damned mysterious. Why not tell me what I will read in tomorrow's paper? I was thinking yesterday that you are one of my only three friends left in the whole damned world. The other two being my office manager Hilda, and Mr. Smitherman."

"Smitherman, yah," said Randy. "I saw him on TV the other day when his wheelchair turned over in front of your office. It had to be him because of the watchcap, the white hair hanging beneath it, and especially the bumper sticker they were handing out at the reunion. They stuck a 'DON'T MESS WITH TEXAS' sticker on the back of his wheelchair and decorated my Cadillac with two of them. Then I picked up half a dozen more in the can at the club where we had the reunion. Guess people dumped them there."

"A half dozen?"

"Yah, they're in the back seat of the car right now. I'm going to give one to my wife for her car if she wants one and will probably throw the others away."

"For some reason, Smitherman wants another bumper sticker like that. You know how people get when they are old. He has mentioned it at least a dozen times to me or Hilda. He's living with me now. Ran away from the Care Center. They thought he was going to a World War II reunion, but I have an idea he never did show up there. Rode three different buses out of Chicago to find my office. He got a bad bump on his head when he fell, but his mind is clear and except for some of his funny ideas, he is good company."

"You can have all five," Randy said. "Let me dump you off back by your office and you can give them to Mr. Smitherman. I'm not getting out of the car, because if those damn TV cameras are still around there on that food tampering story, it would be just my luck to get my picture splattered all over Chicago. I think there is one way we can talk on the phone. I'll call you within a day or two, but we will have to use the language we invented and used on each other in junior high."

"Yaygoo maygeen Laygataygan Agaraygab?" Will brightened at the prospect of reusing the old language they invented in junior high school. No one else in the class could figure it out. And it was so simple. He and Randy invented it as a simulated archaeological dig assignment when they had an outdoor unit, taught by a budding anthropologist from the University. They had to create a culture, invent a language and have a form of Rosetta Stone so the classmates could piece together the various artifacts to understand the values of the represented culture, in addition to giving hints at what caused the death of the culture. Probably next to the paired pairs assignment from Smitherman, it was the most interesting school assignment he ever had, including his college and dental school days.

"Yaygess," smiled Randy, "Aygai waygil caygall yaygoo and gaygive yaygoo agay naygumbager, thaygen yaygoo cagan caygall. The stupid feds won't have an idea in hell what we are talking about, and we could probably detail a murder in our language and get away with it."

The two of them had labeled their language "Latin Arab," differing from Pig Latin, but no more difficult to master. All you had to do to speak Latin Arab was to sound each consonant in a word, follow it with an "AYG" sound (except for final consonant sounds) and keep it consistent. For example, "Will" became "Waygill," "Shit on Chad" became "Shaygit aygon Chaygad," and "School sucks" became "Skaygool Saygucks." The entire simulated dig assignment had been a blast for both of them, and they had occasionally broken into the language in high school when they wanted to share a secret in front of others, or more often to utter derogatory remarks about people they happened to be with at the time.

As Randy dropped off Will at the mall he said, "You will get a call in a day or two telling you where and when we'll have the money meeting. Don't worry about a thing. Everything will turn out OK for you, and with your help, things will be OK for us too. Read the news first and it will clue you in."

Back at the office Will carried his five DON'T MESS WITH TEXAS bumper stickers into the X-ray room where Smitherman was peacefully sleeping. Will carefully placed the stickers on the wheel chair where Smitherman would be certain to see them, scribbled a note, "Santa was early this year," went into the adjoining room and changed into his pajamas before reclining in Chair Number 2 for the night.

After exchanging greetings with Smitherman the next morning, Will said, "After coffee and before Hilda gets here, let's take a little spin around the parking lot. I need to get a newspaper or two. We have been sort of out of it the last few days. By the way, Asa, is there any chance that the Care Center people saw you on TV when you first got here?"

Will wheeled Asa through the lot as Asa struck his customary pose, bandage on head, watchcap, head slumped to his chest, appearing to all onlookers as one truly pushing death. How he could speak distinctly in that position was a mystery to Will, but Asa's answer was clear.

"Very unlikely. From what I have gathered, the photographers were from WGN, which does transmit throughout the country, but you don't get it unless you are hooked up with a Cable Television Network. The Care Center has no cable, and we confine our television watching to exactly four local stations. Not a chance, unless someone at the reunion saw me, but if they had, we would have heard about it by now. Believe me, Will, I have been thinking about that possibility, too, and have been prepared to hide out in your clinic or the chiropractors next door should anyone come around looking for me. I'm not going back there. Right now I'm having the time of my life and plan to keep it that way."

After purchasing a Chicago Tribune from a dispensing machine, Will pushed the wheelchair with one hand while holding the Tribune with the other. As Randy had predicted, there was a front-page story about a Muzafer (Gus) Harrigian, who had been released on a million-dollar bond throughout his trial, but was facing up to twelve charges, any one of which could sentence him to Joliet or Leavenworth for the remainder of his life.

Muzafer Harrigian must be Randy's father-in-law, thought Will. No wonder he said they had a "little problem." My God, three murder charges, extortion, attempted bribery, violation of the Mann Act, illegal distribution of drugs, just for starters.

From the article Will gathered that the trial would be winding down within the month, and barring intervention from a divine power especially partial to members of AAAA, Ltd., the verdict would be guilty on most counts.

This information came as a shock to Will. Unlike the name of Capone, which was a household word in every Chicago and suburban neighborhood, hardly anyone had ever seen the name of Muzafer Harrigian in print. And Randy was married to Muzafer's daughter! "Sort of a family business," Randy had mentioned at the reunion. "I guess so," thought Will.

Chapter 6

THE MEETING

At 9:15 that evening, just as it was getting dark, Will pulled his van into the little side street in front of Greek Island and was hailed to a stop by a tall, hungry-looking Greek youth, dressed in a uniform somewhat too large for him.

"Keys, mister. Valet Sorvice. Parka car. Real Safe."

Will wondered by the accent how many days or weeks the young man had been in this country, but he reluctantly handed over the keys, entered the main restaurant, and located a rather uncomfortable bench where people waited to be seated. Before he got settled, he spotted Randy, walking to the cash register from the restaurant. Also noticeable were three men standing, strategically situated throughout the restaurant. Although they were dressed in the costume of FBI agents, Will had a hunch they were not. But whoever they were, he thought it best to avoid their searching eyes, and to pretend not to notice them.

"I knew you'd be early," said Randy. "Anybody follow you?"

"No. Apparently, they can't get in here without using the valet service, and no one was behind me at all. Is your father-in-law here?"

"He never goes into public places, but two other guys are here and they can take care of your problems for you. You don't have a thing to worry about. Trust me."

Randy led Will to a table for four, where two older men were sipping Ouzo, while playing some type of numbers game to see which one would get stuck with the bill.

"This is the guy I told you about," said Randy to the two men. "Will, meet Nick and Al. Two of AAAA Ltd's best men. My father-in-law says both of them can speak for him and for you to trust them implicitly."

Will wondered how long Randy had been using words like "implicitly" because he had not been as interested in words as such people as Smitherman and himself. But, thought Will, people do develop a lot after graduating from high school. As Smitherman used to say, "It's all a matter of motivation."

"Ouzo, Will?" asked Nick. "Good, no ice. Real Greeks never put ice in ouzo or ouzo on ice. Fucks up the flavor. You a Greek boy, Willy? I didn't think so. To the point. How much you need and how good you are as a dentist?"

"It's a lot, so much that I'm hesitant to say."

"Well, we know. But you smart not to talk too much. Don't admit nothing. You need half a mill. You earn it if you're good dentist."

"I don't know how I could earn that much soon enough to pay my debts," said Will. "But anything will help."

"Nothin' to worry 'bout," said Nick. And to Al, "Tell Willy about our organization so he don't worry too much."

"Hokay," chimed in Al, as though anticipating the request. Speaking from memory, and as devoid of thought process as most TV news commentators, Al complied, "AAAA is a multicultural, non-sexist, equal opportunity employer, meeting all federal standards of nondiscrimination and worker safety. We are or will be completely legit by the year 2000. Our mission is to help the homeless, eradicate AIDS, employ the handicapped, stop the flow of drugs, promote patriotism, make America number one in education, and clean up the slums. You come work for us Willy, and we add to our goals, 'make everybody's teeth pretty.' Hokay?"

If Will had learned anything back at SUI High, it was to be a good listener, and the terms "multicultural" and "non-sexist" demanded an ex-planation, if only to prove to Al that he had listened to his spiel about AAAA.

"Multicultural?" Will asked. "You have minorities in AAAA?"

"Betcher ass we do," said Al. "Back in the 30's all they had in the Capone gang were Dagos, that means Italian today, and all the government had to do to send Capone up was to find one non-Italian fed, more interested in publicity than in cooperating with the people, and they found a son of a bitch named Elliott Ness. After that it was Capone's ass."

"Too bad, too, added the AAAA spokesperson, but good for us. We've got a hundred per cent multicultural organization now, except we are missing a few Blacks, Orientals, and Jews. And of course, no Turks are allowed, because of what they did to the boss's grandparents back in Armenia before World War I."

"How about non-sexist?" Asked Will.

"You mean do we got women in AAAA? Sure. Just like the American Legion. We have more than 100 women in the AAAA auxiliary. They bake pies, visit orphans, widows, and nursing homes, sing in church choirs, all that shit. Our goal is to be 100% American, just like the Chamber of Commerce and the Republican Party. And Willy," Al concluded, as he downed his third Ouzo, "we're getting there. And you can help."

"I will," promised Will. "I need the money."

"You like beezeball?" Nick appeared to change the subject, to Will's distress. He didn't even know what beezeball was, fearing it would turn out to be more powerful than ouzo. And he had to drive back to the office that evening.

"Gus wants to know if you are a baseball fan," explained Randy. "We often do business at Wrigley Field. We like to pick a sunny afternoon, and we stay off camera by sitting in the box seats. The cameras are always looking through the bleachers for scantily clad women with big tits, so there is no chance of anyone seeing us on TV. The box seats in Wrigley Field are the safest place in Chicago to pull off business transactions."

"Yes, sir," agreed Will, smiling at the 'big tit' part of Randy's explanation, yet responding to the question at hand, "I've been a Cubs fan most of my life. Just about everyone where I grew up followed the Cubs. Except for those who ignored baseball completely. Which was most of them. It was a college town. People in college towns care more about college football than anything else in the world. The world could end tomorrow, but if the Hawkeyes could beat Minnesota, everybody would be happy."

Nick thought that was a hell of a long speech for a sober man and attributed it to Will's refill of ouzo. "That's powerful stuff if you're not a Greek boy," he said.

Turning to Randy, he added. "Your friend is hookay. We talk at ball game. You make arrangements. Got to go now. Business."

Will feared he had blown the prospect of getting the loan, as Nick and Al departed, but Randy, sensing his trepidation, said. "Everything will be OK. They like you. You will get your money, in return for a small favor."

"What's that?"

Randy looked around, making sure the waiter could not overhear, and whispered, "Wraygalaygee Faygield taygomaygarago," which translated to "Wrigley Field tomorrow."

Then he handed Will a box-seat ticket behind first base, saying, "Be there, buddy. And study the X-rays in this envelope. You have a half-million piece of dental work to do. I'll call you tomorrow."

The combination of the ouzo, the prospect of so much money, and the feeling that there was something slightly illegal about the situation he was letting himself be dragged into, gave Will a rather woozy feeling during the entire drive back to his office. He recalled a line from Faust, something about "At first you are free, but after the first step you are a slave."

But what else was there to do, he asked himself as he studied the X-rays, while propped up on a pillow in his office. The X-rays showed 14 real teeth, two with root canals. Also, there were two small bridges. Not too unusual for an X-ray, he decided. Will wondered why the X-rays were so important.

When Will got up the next morning, no one was in the office, but he saw a note from Hilda next to the hot plate where he brewed his instant coffee.

"Don't look for the van because I have Asa in it. Last night he said he wanted to see the Brookfield Zoo, so I'm taking him out for breakfast on the way. You were sleeping so soundly I didn't have the heart to wake you up. All is well. We'll be back before noon. OK?"

Because it was already nine o'clock and patients were certain to show up any minute, Will prepared for a morning without an assistant by readying his equipment. But there were no dental patients.

Stepping outside to see why it was so quiet in the office, he saw a sign, "Open at 1:00 p.m."

That seemed to explain it.

Inside, the phone rang, probably an emergency patient, Will thought.

But it was Randy, speaking in Latin Arab. Translated it turned out to be. "Game starts at 1:30 today. All systems on go."

"Holy moon landing, Batman. You're talking like an astronaut instead of a mobster," said Will, in the same coded language. "I'll be there." He amended the "open at 1:00 p.m." sign to read "Open tomorrow," showered, shaved, put on his Cubs hat, and prepared for an afternoon at Wrigley Field.

Mid July is rarely good for the Cubs, thought Will. Year after year the radio and TV announcers predict a great season for the Cubs when they are in spring training. Then it is all downhill. He could count the years when Harry Caray's favorite line in April was "If the Cubs win today, they will be tied for first place." In May it changed to, "Only three games out of first. If the Cubs sweep the Mets and if the Pirates and Cardinals lose their next two games, we will be tied for first." By June Caray was less optimistic, changing it to "By winning the next two, the Cubs will be at 500."

But now it was the middle of July, and the most optimistic Cubs fan could only hope that if they beat Montreal four times in succession, they would no longer be alone in the cellar of the National League East. Smitherman had mentioned more than once that in the old days when they had only eight teams in the League, and no East-West divisions, "next to last" meant seventh place. But the way the announcers explained it today, fifth place in the Eastern Division seemed to be a great improvement over the old days, even though there were at least 10 or 11 National League teams with a better record than the Cubs.

But win or lose, the Cubs continued to draw near-capacity crowds at Wrigley, partly because the seating capacity was considerably less than that of other major league parks. And when they boasted of "a million total attendance already this year," they were ignoring the fact that some stadiums had drawn three million.

"Oh, well," thought Will. "I would go watch the Cubs anyway. Even if no one was giving me half a million dollars." So with the prospect of so much cash coming in, Will took a cab to Wrigley Field, tipped the driver generously, ate lunch in a neighborhood bar, and was in his box seat a half-hour before game time.

The seats on either side of him were empty until two Chicago Tribune "employees of the month" appeared behind the pitcher's mound to sing the National Anthem. Then a powerfully built man, of about 55 or 60 years of age, seated himself at Will's left, just as the announcer said, "Ladies and Gentlemen please rise and join us in singing the Star Spangled Banner."

"Good day for a game, Will," said the man, as both stood and listened to the singing. "I'm Raphael. Thank God we're not playing Montreal, because then those tone-deaf bastards out there would sing two anthems. Seems strange to me, but you never see a Canadian baseball player, though they sing that Canadian anthem wherever the team goes. It would make more sense to sing the Mexican National Anthem, or the Dominican Republic's, that's where the players come from. But nobody gives a shit, right Will?"

Will, wanting to be agreeable, but not knowing what to say, nodded his head, then noting a scowl on Raphael's face, immediately quit nodding and shook his head. He didn't know which way to move his head to indicate concurrence with Raphael's remark. He hated comments like "nobody cares, right?" because he didn't know what to do with his head. There should be some type of circular motion, he thought, to show complete agreement with a negative statement.

"We'll talk baseball till the 7th inning, if we talk at all," mumbled Raphael, without really opening his mouth. "If there happens to be a good-looking broad near us, the TV people might aim their goddam cameras this way and there would be half a million people trying to read our lips. It's OK to talk during the 7th inning stretch, though, because the camera picks up only Harry Caray when he sings 'Take me out to the Ball Game.' That's sort of a horseshit song, too, especially the way he sings it."

Will nodded again and wished Raphael would get to the real point of the ball game. Specifically, the half million dollars and what he needed to do to earn that much. Perhaps, thought Will, Wrigley Field was a good spot for someone with a work ethic to ease his conscience, because the Cubs were carrying a lot of players and paying them well over a million dollars, sometimes two or three, for not really doing anything. A good month's work for a Cubs pitcher was one inning's work, getting knocked out of the box, followed by four weeks on the disabled list. All at once Will felt that he deserved a half million just to put up with a team like that. He felt better as he suffered through six and a half innings in complete silence.

Then came the seventh inning stretch. Will and Raphael were mouthing "Take Me Out To The Ball Game," when he felt Raphael press something into his hand. It felt like a key. And without looking, he knew it was when Raphael sang into his ear, "It's one, two, three flights downstairs at the old Union Station." Then Raphael departed.

The game mercifully ended, four hours after it had begun. The Cubs lost, and Will hailed a cab for the Union Station. Inside the station he had no problem in locating the locker, which contained a Chicago Cubs overnight bag. Removing the bag ("It is heavy, but I won't look now," thought Will), he took another cab back to the dental office.

When he arrived he saw Randy standing in front of the office door.

"Anything wrong?" Will asked.

"Just the opposite. Bring the bag to the car and we'll take a look at it. OK?"

Inside Randy's Cadillac, they both examined the contents. Will had never seen so many $50 bills in his life.

"I don't understand," said Will. "It's great, but I can't believe this is happening. What now?"

"Do you trust me?" Randy asked.

"Well, I have exactly three friends in the world, you, Hilda and Asa. If I can't trust you, I might as well hang it up. But what do I do?"

"In a day or two you will be hearing from me again. I'll need the van and I'll take Smitherman with me. I want him to meet my kids. Also give Hilda an advance and the rest of the week off. Tomorrow night or the next night you and I are going to be busy. Study those X-rays and meet your new temporary dental assistant. Me."

He held out his hand. They shook.

Inside the office Asa and Hilda were taking turns at the computer, playing Klondike, a solitaire game, to be sure, but the way the computer game worked, each player earned a score, so the two were happily competing for high scores. Hilda was controlling the mouse, and Will knew it was not a good time to talk to her because she was racing against time. Every few seconds wasted would lower the score on the old Alaska gold rush game of solitaire.

As the two of them were ignoring Will, he opened the safe and after removing a few thousand dollars from the Cubs bag, placed it inside, near the back. He seldom kept any secrets from either Hilda or Asa, but he knew this must be an exception. And the only part of the secret he knew was that he was a half-million dollars richer than he had been the day before. Some day he would know why, he hoped. Or dreaded, as the case might be.

"Good to see you back." said Hilda. "Asa's cleaning me. Says I owe him $800 just on points in the last five games."

Asa looked up proudly, saying, "Not bad hands for 85 years old. Would you agree, Will? Want to play for a dime a point?"

"No, I surrender," said Will. "How would you two like to go out and eat?"

They both agreed.

"Where to," asked Will. "Asa, I'll let you decide if you forfeit your claim to the $800 Hilda doesn't have."

Instantly Asa answered, "At a Bob Evans. We ate in one on the way to Memphis. Their biscuits and gravy are easy for me to chew."

"Where's the nearest one," asked Will.

Hilda said she didn't know for sure where the nearest one was, but they had one in Joliet, if he didn't mind traveling a few extra miles, so the three of them got into the van, with Hilda at the wheel.

Will pretended to pay attention to the conversation on the way to Joliet, but he couldn't get his mind off the half million. He wondered if he would one day become a permanent nonvoting resident of Joliet. As he recalled, that was where they sent Nathan Leopold and his partner after their crime and trial.

In the restaurant they asked for a smoking section, because of Asa's Chesterfield addiction, and they were seated between the restrooms and a cart for dirty dishes.

After they were seated, Asa said, "I don't believe I would want a community named after me, because one never knows how it will turn out. Take Joliet, for example. They named it in honor of the famous explorer, Louis Jolliet, and even though they misspelled it, it is an insult to a great man. Look at it now. Just a prison town, making the news only when there are attempted escapes or riots. I would not want a prison town named after me."

"Right," said Hilda. "They should rename it Reagan. Ronnie is Illinois' own pride and joy, but he wouldn't even let his presidential library be this far from Hollywood. Every Republican in Illinois would be honored to have a community named after their native son. And the Democrats would enjoy seeing headlines reading, 'Criminal sentenced to Reagan.' It is not fair to Joliet. Reagan perhaps, or Nixon or Bush, but not Joliet."

As the three stopped at the cash register on the way out, Asa asked for one of those cards to fill out and place in the suggestion box. He wrote "Excellent biscuits and gravy. But the name of your city is misspelled. Louis Jolliet had two 'L' s' in his name."

Back at the office the next morning, Randy called, and Will decoded his Latin-Arab message as, "Be there this afternoon to pick up Asa and Hilda. I will need your van but am bringing you a car to use when they are with me."

It was a most busy day at the office, with dental patients arriving every few minutes, beginning at 8:30. Hilda had made several phone calls, apologizing for the closed office the day before, and many of the cancellations arrived, after a promise of a discount for their inconvenience. Will had never understood the ramifications of placing a sign on the door, reading, "Closed until tomorrow," or words to that effect. Hilda had proved herself a most excellent business manager.

"When you are at Randy's with Asa today, I am counting on you to pay our most pressing back bills. I do have some cash, more than you will believe," said Will. "Don't ask any questions, please, but take the books and the Cubs overnight bag I put in the safe today and ask Randy to help you pay bills and deposit the rest where it will be safe. One thing for certain, AAAA knows how to invest without seeming to break the law, and I'll need all the help I can get."

"Of course, I'll do what needs to be done," answered Hilda. "And I won't ask any questions, now or later, about where the money came from. Does Randy know?"

"Yes, he knows everything. A lot more than I do. All I know is that I have a lot of borrowed money, with a chance to earn it before having to pay it back. That's all I know. Believe me."

"Be careful," said Hilda. "I like Randy, but it worries me a little that he never seems to give a damn about anything. Thinks his life is charmed. Maybe you can make him be a little more careful, too."

Chapter 7

THE PATIENT

Randy drove a new Toyota into the mall parking lot at 3:30 that afternoon, went into Will's office and asked Hilda, "Ready? Oh, yes, better bring an overnight bag. We'll be gone for a couple of weeks."

"Two weeks!" Will echoed, "Hilda, can you clear our appointment calendar?"

"I sure can," she said. "Will I be near a phone, Randy?"

"Anything you want," said Randy. "How soon will you be ready to go?" He glanced at his watch.

"I'm ready," Hilda said, "already packed." Hilda loved to travel, no matter where to or when.

"I am ready, also," Asa responded. "Should I walk or take the wheelchair?"

"Wheelchair," said Randy. "By all means. If you don't need it, believe me, we do. Let's go. And Will, here are the Toyota keys, and an AAAA credit card. But stay close by. If you don't see me tonight, you will tomorrow. Some details have to be ironed out. Study your X-rays."

Will watched them pull out of the parking lot five minutes later, and took another look at the X-rays. They were simple enough. Two crowns, two bridges, four extractions, and two root canals. A person could memorize an elementary X-ray of that limited complexity without ever seeing the inside of a dental school.

With the office empty at 4:45, Will, keyring in hand, was about to lock the doors and go somewhere nearby to eat, when his one-time patient, Patrick O'Shea, Hilda's ex-husband walked in.

"Hey, Doc," said Patrick, "got time to look at my tooth?"

"Of course," answered Will, putting his keyring beside the office phone. "Is it bothering you?"

"No, but I was in the neighborhood and thought I would drop in. Where's Hilda?"

"She's gone. Needed a vacation." Will omitted any details that would assist Patrick in his stalking of Hilda.

"Where's the old man with the wheelchair?" Patrick asked, as he climbed into the dentist's chair.

"Not sure," Will lied, "said something about Wrigley Field or just visiting one of his favorite neighborhoods on the south side of Chicago. Do the Cubs play tonight?" He hoped to distract Patrick by getting him to talk about the Cubs.

"So, it's just you and me, huh, Doc?"

"For today, at least," said Will, looking over the tooth he had capped, and thinking it quite remarkable that he and Patrick had two things in common. They both were very well acquainted with Hilda, and they had teeth that when X-rayed, could pass for clones.

"Don't you think it's time I X-rayed your teeth?" Will asked.

"No, I ain't about to get no X-ray. I heard they can give you radioactive poisoning, cause sterility, and give AIDS to people. I read that somewhere when I was working downstate."

"Well, we won't X-ray them then," said Will. "When were you downstate?" He wouldn't tell Patrick, of course, but the term "downstate," referring to all of Illinois south of Chicago, was what Smitherman would have called "altitudinally incorrect" because Chicago was lower in altitude than was Southern Illinois. Upstate New York, by contrast, according to Smitherman, was altitudinally accurate, because New York City was virtually at sea level, while the rest of New York State was higher.

"For the past two weeks, between Peoria and Danville," Patrick answered. "I work for the Illinois Highway Department. Won't get laid off neither, because they are always repairing highways and only three people in the department are experts with explosives. That's one good thing I got out of Nam. Learned how to blow things up. But I'm going to quit."

"Too dangerous?" Asked Will.

"Hell no, I'm going into the explosive business for myself."

Will recalled a story he had heard from an old professor in dental school about the merits of working for others or going into business for oneself. It concerned a small county seat in the Old South, and involved a person called in those days "The Village Idiot." The civic leaders, trying to give the so-called Village Idiot some pride and a tiny income, had hired him to polish the cannon in front of the Court House. He performed this function every day for 25¢ per day, providing him with spending money, while at the same time keeping him busy and out of trouble. This went on for some time, the professor had related, until one day the cannon polisher walked into the council meeting and said, "I quit."

"Why?" the county supervisor had asked.

"I'm tired of working for other people. I'm buying my own cannon and going into business for myself," he responded.

This story by the professor had been followed by a dutiful round of student guffaws, as Will recalled.

But back to the present. "You're positive about no X-rays?" asked Will. "Most everybody has some on file. I don't want to argue with the people in Peoria and Danville, but to my knowledge a dental X-ray has never caused anyone a problem. The old man you mentioned went most of his life without an X-ray, but we took one. Know what we found?"

"What?" queried Patrick.

"The head of a diamond drill embedded beneath where he once had a twelve-year molar. Some dentist left it there when he was extracting a tooth, had to break it up to get the root out, and lost the diamond head in there."

"Is it valuable?" asked Patrick. "Hell, the old man could be worth more than you could give him credit for, riding around in that wheelchair. Who gets it when he croaks?"

"The wheelchair?" asked Will.

"Christ no, the diamond. Who gets it? We had guys in Nam with fruit jars full of valuable dental work. Carried pliers around with them all the time, pulling gold teeth out of dead Nams. Hell, some of them went home rich. Who gets the old man's diamond when he dies?"

"It's an industrial diamond," said Will. "Not too valuable, but at least if he gets mugged, robbed and killed tonight cruising around Chicago, they will be able to figure out who he is just by checking his dental records."

"That's another reason I don't want any X-rays," said Patrick, getting out of the chair, "When I get blown away, I don't want the cops to figure out who I was. Why make it easy for them?"

"Say, Doc," changing the subject, "Can I use your phone?"

"Right in there," said Will, arranging the chair area. "Local call?"

"Hell, yes," said Patrick, heading for the phone.

If Will had one weakness, it was that he trusted people too much. He really believed that Patrick wanted to use the phone, and in a way, Patrick did use it, twisting apart the mouthpiece and deftly inserting a disc inside, allowing him to tap Will's office phone. He would find out what Hilda was up to, all right, and maybe beat her up a time or two before he went back to Peoria to blow up some more of the Everett Dirksen Freeway.

And if Will had two weaknesses, the other was carelessness with his own private property, such as his office key on the key ring where he had placed it earlier, in plain sight, right beside the phone.

After tapping the phone, Patrick picked up the keys, yelled, "Thanks a lot," and headed out the door toward the neighboring True Value Hardware outlet, where he duplicated the three keys on the ring. The entire operation took less than ten minutes, after which he came back into Will's office, returned the original key ring, and again departed while Will was still tinkering in the patient area.

Early the next morning Patrick was seated in his Chevy pickup, with the phone to his ear, monitoring the calls to Will's office, hoping to learn the whereabouts of Hilda. It was virtually impossible for a passer-by to see Patrick in the pickup because of the dark tinted windows on both sides and in the back. Viewers from the front of the pickup could see only a mammoth smiling face on a huge sunshade spread across the windshield. The smiling face was the type used by elementary teachers to motivate their kids if they ever did anything right. Only about 100 times bigger. From all appearances, the pickup looked to be that of one of the employees in the mall, perhaps a kindergarten or first grade teacher with a summer job at a checkout counter.

On the reverse side of the sunshade, a message read, "Send Help," but since there is no record of anyone ever paying attention to a "send help" sunscreen sign, Patrick's pickup was perfectly inconspicuous in the mall, even when it announced "Send Help" to all who viewed it from the front.

Patrick somehow believed he could get Hilda to change her mind about leaving him, while wondering if anything was going on between her and Will Mosley. He didn't think there was anything between the two, because in his mind Will and Hilda had only the dental practice in common. No one in the world would prefer Will to himself, thought Patrick, as a few routine calls came to Will's office, all by patients apparently.

The call that set Patrick to thinking came in at about 10:00. He heard Will answer "Dentist," and from the other end, just gibberish, sounding like "Taygonaygite Tayggen." To add to the confusion the short message was repeated, coming out "Taygonaygite Taygen. Taygonaygite Taygen." He told himself he would have to look into that because he hadn't heard language like that since he served in Nam. Patrick did not like it, but the voice that uttered the mysterious message was certainly not Hilda's. It was a man's voice. And on Will's end of the line, nothing was said at all. Just the click you hear when someone hangs up.

Patrick told himself to look into the matter of Taygonaygite Taygen, thinking perhaps that it was a new type of aluminum siding advertised over the phone. He himself had been the recipient of some weird telemarketing messages in the past couple of years, often thinking it was some boyfriend trying to call Hilda, but upon Patrick's answering the phone, merely pretended to be selling something.

Maybe this "Taygonaygite Taygen" guy was trying to get into Hilda's pants, thought Patrick, but why would he talk gibberish to Will? Hilda did not belong to Will, did she? Hell, no. She belonged to himself, Patrick O'Shea. And as soon as he saw her, you could bet your ass he was going to make her sorry for messing up his life since she walked out on him. But where was she really?

He complimented himself on his skill in obtaining their office key and tapping the phone. They would be hearing some more from Patrick O'Shea, he told himself, as he removed the sunscreen and drove to McDonald's, partly for something to eat, but mostly for the use of their men's room.

Meanwhile, in the dental office, Will was caring for a waiting room full of patients, and doing it without an assistant, hoping he would not be suffering from fatigue by ten o'clock that evening. He automatically knew that "Taygonaygite Tayggen" simply meant "Tonight Ten."

Closing the office at 5:00 p.m., Will went out for a sandwich, not noticing the Chevy Pickup with the tinted windows and the smiling face in front. And if he had noticed, he would have thought little of it. Even though the smiling face was facing east as sundown approached, it would not have concerned Will, because he was thinking about what was going to happen tonight at ten o'clock.

After a bite to eat Will spent the next couple of hours studying and memorizing the X-ray while watching the Cubs on WGN. Although the X-ray became boring to look at after studying it so many times, it was a shade more exciting than the Cubs game. The Cubs were now battling it out for last place in the National League East and playing at Montreal. If the Cubs win tonight, Harry Caray had announced, they will be a full game ahead of the Expo's and only 21 games out of first place, with all of August and September to catch up with the leaders. It could be done, but it was not likely, Will thought, as he turned off the TV at 9:50 with the Cubs trailing 11 to nothing.

Just then Patrick, seated in his pickup, hoping for phone calls to monitor, noticed the Dodge van pull into the parking lot, stopping just a few feet away from Patrick's pickup. He saw Hilda emerge from the driver's seat, walk to the passenger side, open the sliding doors, and push the button that would lower the old man in the wheelchair.

Before the wheelchair, complete with passenger, had touched the ground, Patrick used the better part of his vocabulary in yelling, "There you are, you bitch, whore, slut." and grabbed Hilda from behind.

He could hardly believe what happened next. Hilda must have taken some self-defense lessons in one of those feminist gymnasiums, because Patrick took a hard left to the nose, staggered, and then suffered a haymaker on the chin, decking him on the asphalt between the van and his pickup. The next thing he knew, someone had lifted him up and tossed him into the pickup cab, where he was clobbered on the back of the head with a policeman's sap, one of those utensils Chicago police use when they do not want to leave too many marks on their victims.

Hilda must have been considerate, however, thought Patrick, when he awakened several hours later, because she had reversed the sunshade on the windshield so an observer from the outside would no longer see the smiling face, but rather a message, "Send Help."

"Maybe she still loves me," thought Patrick.

The entire episode in the parking lot took no more than a minute and a half, and Will missed the whole show, getting to the office door seconds too late.

As he opened the door to let the two in, he asked, "Hilda, what happened? Asa, what's wrong?" Hilda did not look quite the same to him outside in the nearly vacant shopping center, and Asa certainly appeared to have taken a turn for the worse, head bandaged, and body slumped over to a greater extent than he had ever been since he left the nursing home.

"I'm not Hilda," said the person pushing the wheelchair, removing his wig and kicking off his high heels. "And this is not Asa. Come on, we've got work to do and I'm your new temporary assistant. What the hell kind of neighborhood is this anyway? Some bastard out front tried to mug me and I had to coldcock him. He'll live though, which is more than you can say for your patient here. Let's get his teeth fixed before rigor mortis sets in."

"Want me to call the police about the attempted mugging?"

"Funny," replied Randy, getting the corpse ready to hoist from the wheelchair. "All we need here tonight is a roomful of cops. With people watching, it would be a real challenge to pull this operation off."

Still thinking of the disguise, Will said, "God, you said you were into community theatre, but I didn't know you were this good at stage makeup. Up close you don't look much like Hilda at all, but you would have to know her pretty well to tell the difference."

Will and Randy hoisted the corpse into chair #3, deciding it would be easier to work with in a dental chair than in the wheelchair. And except for one or two days in the past few weeks, Chair #3 had been unoccupied. Randy ripped off the bandages.

From habit Will talked to his patients. That was why so many people preferred him to other dentists. Not that the rest of them tortured in silence, but because Will really knew what to say and when to say it. He never took a patient by surprise but told them every move he was about to make, subscribing to the theory that if you know what is coming you will be prepared. Also, he hated the idea of inflicting pain on his patients, often to the extreme.

For example, upon seating Asa's double in the chair, Will automatically prepared a needle-load of Novocaine in order to make the impending complex operation as painless as possible.

"You can't hurt him, even if you try," chuckled Randy. "Just fix him up like the X-ray and let me get him the hell out of here. That son of a bitch in the parking lot will be coming to in four or five hours, and I would rather not have to kill him. The only reason for destroying a life is to make another person's life better. That's what my father-in-law always says. And I am trying to be just as compassionate as he is."

"I'm sure you are," said Will, handing him a pair of rubber gloves. "Put these on and we'll get started."

"Why the hell should I wear gloves?" asked Randy.

"So we won't get AIDS, or give it to the patient."

"Well, this guy won't bleed, and you can bet your ass he won't sue you if he gets AIDS in here." But Randy put on the gloves.

Will began the operation by preparing to extract the two necessary teeth for a match, and from long habit said, "OK, open wide, please."

Randy, wearing the rubber gloves said, "OK, just to humor you, and opened his own mouth as wide as possible."

"Not you, him," said Will. "You'll have to hold his mouth open. Do it with these pliers. Just stick them in there so his mouth will stay open."

Randy complied, as Will pulled the two teeth.

"I guess I'll take those with me when I leave," said Randy. "The boss likes to see things like this. It's like how we used to bring the front feet of gophers to the Johnson County Court House when we were kids to collect our 10¢ bounty. Each two front feet proved that all was over for that particular gopher. Remember?"

"Yes, now to two, I believe, basic root canals to match the X-ray."

Will searched around the cabinet for no more than a few seconds and held something in his hand.

"What's that?" asked Randy.

"Rubber dam. Keeps saliva from working its way into the hole I'm going to leave when I remove the nerve. Prevents infection."

"For Christ's sake, infection is the last thing you need to worry about tonight," complained Randy.

"Well, call it habit then," said Will. "It's the only way I have ever done a root canal. In dental school they always said, 'use a rubber dam' and that's what I need to do."

After securing the rubber dam on the first tooth of the root canal duo, Will noticed that the corpse's tongue was interfering with his view of the tooth, so he said, almost automatically, "Lift your tongue up, please. To the roof of the mouth."

Randy complied, lifting his own tongue to the roof of his mouth.

"No, his tongue," said Will. "Hold it up out of the way."

"You got any superglue?"

"Over here," answered Will. "Have you used it before?"

"Once to fix my father-in-law's rocking chair," said Randy. "I'm a fast learner, too."

After Randy glued the patient's tongue to the hard palate, giving Will free access to his work, the next steps went off smoothly, interrupted only by Will's changing the rubber dam from one tooth to the next, until the root canals would match the X-ray.

"Now for a few basic fillings," said Will, as he prepared the necessary solutions on his Bunsen burner. We'll be done pretty soon. How about that guy in the pickup? Are you sure he won't come to before two a.m.?"

"Positive," said Randy. "You've got your skills, I've got mine. He'll feel no pain for at least two more hours."

An hour later, the corpse's teeth were coming very close to matching those on the mysterious X-ray, so Will said to Randy, "We've got one more thing to do. Just to make certain."

"What's that?"

"Get an X-ray. We'll have to haul him over there," pointing to a tiny alcove surrounded by curtains, similar to what you see in a clothing store, where you go to try on a pair of pants.

"OK, I'm with you," said Randy, holding up the corpse by the feet and legs. "Take the top and when I say 'three,' lift. Just like one of those football plays at SUI high. Right?"

With the patient tied to a stool in the X-ray room, Will prepared for the X-ray by asking Randy, "Hand me that bib, there, OK?"

"He's not hungry," said Randy.

"No, the X-ray apron. Looks like a bib. We tie it on to patients, like a bullet proof vest."

"Somebody going to try to shoot him?" asked Randy.

"No, but it absorbs the radioactivity from the X-rays. It is common knowledge that for some individuals, multiple X-ray exposure can cause cancer."

"This guy won't get cancer," said Randy, wondering if Will was beginning to lose it. "And if he does, he won't ever know about it."

Will forgot about the protective bib, asked Randy to step aside, and turned on the mobile X-ray camera, which swept back and forth in front of the patient while photographing the dentures.

"Now, in a minute or so, we'll develop this and see if we have a match."

Five minutes later, while comparing the new X-ray with the old one Will had been given at Greek Island, Randy said, "Looks great to me. Can't tell the difference."

"I can. The Greek Island X-ray has pointed canines. They come to a slightly sharper point than the ones on this guy. Let's get him back in the chair. It will only take a minute."

Measuring the width and angle of projection of the Greek Island canines, while using a powerful microscope, Will took a few mental notes and began grinding the ends of the corpse's canines to sharper points until he was satisfied with his work. Then after taking a second X-ray and satisfied that they were as perfect a match as one could find, he handed both X-rays to Randy and said, "Someday I'd certainly like to know what is happening."

"Well, for one thing, you're not broke any more," said Randy, rebandaging the corpse, placing an old navy Watchcap on its head and pushing him out toward the office door. "Now, I'll have to get my Hilda disguise back on and get out of here. I'll call you in a day or two. By the way, here's a book of checks you can fill out and cash at any AAAA bank. They are listed in the Yellow Pages. It's been fun. The last time we worked together on anything like this was in biology class at SUI high when we dissected frogs. My God, you even talked to the dead frogs you worked on back then. You haven't changed a bit. See you," he said as he wheeled the corpse out into the parking lot, put him in the van, took another look at the sleeping bastard in the Chevy pickup, and went on his way. "I think this is going to work," Randy told himself. "That Will is one damned good dentist. Talk about painless dentistry. He really had it mastered tonight."

Chapter 8

THE SKULL

After Randy left the parking lot with both X-rays and the corpse, Will devoted the next hour to cleaning and scrubbing the work area, making sure to rid his office of any evidence of the dead patient Randy had wheeled in three hours before. Will expected the police to barge in with a search warrant at any moment. He was not certain what the charges would be, and to that extent was grateful to Randy for not telling him any more than he had, which was practically nothing.

He had studied nothing in his dental ethics class in college that made it a crime to work on corpses, he rationalized to himself. In fact, in medical schools throughout the world, the students performed many more operations on corpses than they did on live people. It was a way of becoming skilled, starting by giving shots to oranges until gaining the confidence necessary to plunge a needle into the arm of a talking, feeling patient. Perhaps dentists should adopt this policy, although while many people willed their bodies to medical schools, he knew of none who had willed theirs to a dental school. Not even the part of the body of most practical value to a dental student, namely the skull.

Wondering where and how Randy had acquired the fresh corpse just in time for a ten-p.m. appointment, bothered Will more than anything. You do not just walk into a morgue and say, "I need a dead body for a few hours. Show me what you have back here, and I'll select one to take on a demonstration trip. Then if I like it, I'll buy it."

By now it was approaching two a.m., but Will knew it was futile to try to sleep. In his mind he reviewed the events of the past month, wishing he could have changed even one thing along the way. If he had not gone to the class reunion, he wouldn't have seen Randy. But it was impossible to change the past. And if he had stayed home, perhaps Karen would not have taken all their money and gone to Memphis to feed her obsession with Elvis. True, things would be better if he had simply junked the reunion invitation.

But it had been good to meet Smitherman. And Hilda was a big improvement on Karen, he decided as he took two ice cubes from the freezer, dropped them into a glass and filled it to the brim with Cutty Sark. "Forget it," he told himself as he downed half the glass in one swig. Whatever trouble he was in, Randy was in deeper, and to watch Randy, you would think tonight's events were pretty much routine.

He turned on the TV to WGN, knowing there would be no news about a Chicago murder, a stolen corpse, or anything else related to the evening's activities in his office. A John Wayne movie was showing on WGN, and in less than two minutes the Duke had killed six bad guys, helping Will to put his own nefarious acts in proper perspective. "I haven't killed anyone," said Will, feeling the effects of his Scotch. "Never have, never will."

So, despite his traumatic experience with the corpse, Will was asleep in the chair by 2:30 a.m.

Just as Will was falling asleep in the office, Patrick was awakening in his pickup, wondering what had happened. His jaw felt as though it was broken. He sat up, shook his head from side to side to assure himself that he was still alive, and felt his teeth with his hand to see if they were still there. The last time he felt like this, Hilda's brother was the cause, accounting for the only flaw in his dental history. This time it was Hilda herself. The bitch. She would be sorry for this, and so would that old bastard in the wheelchair. And Doc, too, what the hell ever his name was. I'll make him check my teeth again as soon as he opens, he decided.

Patrick tried to recall the strange message he had heard on the tapped phone to see if there might be a connection between the message and Hilda's attacking him five or six hours earlier. "Taygonaygite Tayggen," he mumbled painfully, "I'll bet it's some kind of judo or karate, maybe a new form of Tae Kwon Do. Hell, yes, that's it. Sounds like Japanese to me. That bitch is into Tae Kwon Do."

To allay suspicion, though he awoke with a headache and a miserable outlook on the promises of a new day, Will was up and around with his office doors open by 8:30 a.m. "If I live through this," he told himself, "I'll be able to afford a receptionist, two dental assistants, a new house, and can pay off my debts. But I certainly wish Hilda would show up. I can't hack this alone and we're beginning to lose patients because of our erratic office hours and shortage of help."

His appointment book cleared, no one was scheduled all day, for which he was grateful. But before Will had a chance to enjoy much of an easy day, Patrick O'Shea staggered into the office. He looked worse than he had the day after Hilda's brother ruined his tooth, which resulted in a gold cap.

Patrick's jaw was swollen and a bit black and blue, he needed a shave, his clothes were disheveled, and his eyes were red and teary.

"Pain killer, Doc," whined Patrick. "And check my teeth. They feel like a couple of them are loose."

"Right away," said Will, "Come on back," beckoning to the chair Patrick most recently had sat in. Will hoped he could arrange his schedule so he would seldom, if ever, have to use the corpse's chair. Perhaps Patrick was actually doing him a favor by coming in for emergency treatment. It allowed Will to get his mind on his work, rather than on the previous evening's living nightmare.

"What happened?" he asked, looking into Patrick's painfully open mouth. "Your teeth seem to be OK this time. One or two lowers are a bit loose, but if you don't eat any caramels or tootsie rolls for the next couple of days, you'll be all right. Did you have an accident?"

"You know damned well what happened, Doc. I had a couple of beers yesterday and was minding my own business right after dark when she jumped me with a club or something."

"Who did?" Will asked.

"Who the hell do you think it was? That assistant of yours that is still my goddamned wife. Where is she?"

"Hilda's gone. I thought I told you that the other day. Where did you see her?"

"Right out front. She was hauling the old bastard around in that van of hers. All I wanted was to make things right with her and she attacked me. Yelled something first, I forget what it was, but the next thing I knew I was coming to in my pickup."

"Well," said Will, handing Patrick a small package of sample Tylenol, "the important thing is to take care of that pain. Looks like you will be wearing that bruise for a day or two. Take two of these now and then every four hours until you feel better. Can you come in again next week?"

"Before that," Patrick answered, washing down the two pain pills with a paper cup filled with water. "Quit my job with the Illinois Highway Department so I could take care of things around here. Going home now to get some sleep. Any sleeping pills here, Doc?"

"This particular Tylenol has a codeine additive. You will sleep. In fact, you really shouldn't be driving after those two pills start taking effect. So, I'd say hurry home now, no booze within two hours of taking these pills, you'll be OK. And believe me, Patrick, I really did not see Hilda last night. If she was in the area with Smitherman, she must have taken him over to the ice cream store. She used to do that once in a while, wheel him over in the evening."

The way Patrick saw it, there was something believable about Will. You could tell by looking a person in the eye whether he was lying or not, and Will did not have the look of a liar when he said he had not seen Hilda last night.

"And Patrick," added Will at the door, "I know what it is to have domestic problems. You and I have something in common. My wife left me and if what you say happened really happened, it looks as though Hilda and you are finished. My advice is to forget it and get on with your life. That's what I'm trying to do."

"Bullshit," mumbled Patrick, holding his jaw in his hand, and heading for his pickup and home.

After four long days and nights of hearing nothing about a corpse, an unsolved murder, or any missing person, not to mention any word from Hilda or Asa, Will decided to wait another day or two before calling Randy to see what was going on and what was happening to Hilda and Asa. But he decided against calling from his office phone. It could easily have been tapped. The cool, almost casual manner Randy conveyed when he wheeled in the corpse for dental work, made Will realize that this type of operation for Randy was probably as common as filling a tooth for a dentist. Will could not get his mind off what the two had done. In legal terminology, the very least they could charge Will with was accessory guilt, being an accessory after the fact, what the hell ever that was supposed to mean.

On the fifth night, from long habit, Will was watching the nine o'clock news on WGN when he saw something that chilled him, despite the hot humid evening. One of WGN's 'on-site' reporters was on the South Side of Chicago commenting on a crushed human skull stashed away in a culvert. Neighborhood children had found it and had informed WGN, hoping to cash in on their "Citizen News Tip Award of the Month." Many television stations solicited these news tips, much to the consternation of the Chicago police, who often first learned of Chicago's latest crime while watching the evening news.

"For some macabre reason, known only by the perpetrator of the crime" said the reporter, "attached to the skull was a pair of glasses, impossible to trace because the lenses were plain window glass."

A video close-up of the grinning skull revealed the same teeth Will and Patrick had worked on just days before in the office. The same sharp canines, the exact spaces where teeth were missing, a smashed single-tooth bridge. There was no doubt in Will's mind that the skull belonged to his midnight patient.

With time to kill at the station before the oatmeal commercial and the weather announcements, one of the co-anchors said to the other. "A culvert on Chicago's South Side. Isn't that the spot where Bobbie Franks' body was found?"

The other co-anchor asked, knowledgeably, "You mean the rock star? No, I think he died in a plane crash in Clear Lake, Iowa. Or was it Mason City?"

"No, you're thinking of Buddy Holly," was the first co-anchor's thinly disguised disgusted reply, as he thought, "God, I wish I could get this airhead fired. She has no idea what is going on the world. How the hell can we kill time between commercials with horseshit remarks like hers?"

After the commercial, which showed an old man chopping wood, while talking about what a great thing it is to eat Instant Quaker Oats, saying "Instant Quaker Oatmeal, it's the right thing to do," the cameras returned to the studio.

The first co-anchor said, "Thanks, folks, we just had two phone calls agreeing that Bobbie Franks' body was found on the South Side of Chicago, but don't be alarmed, folks. It was all taken care of, and that was back in May of 1924. The two murderers, Richard (Dickie) Loeb and Nathan (Babe) Leopold both paid for their crimes and neither is any longer a threat to society. Loeb was killed in prison in 1936 and Leopold died in Puerto Rico in 1971. Now to the weather."

Will sat there stunned. He knew Randy was aware that Will watched the nine-p.m. news regularly, and he knew Randy had a sick sense of humor, but those damned glasses on the skull could get them both sent up for life, or at the very least give Will a heart attack. He knew how Randy's mind worked, and the glasses on the skull were proof to Will that he was having fun with the old SUI High School Leopold-Loeb partner assignment. It was a lost pair of prescription glasses that had led the police directly to Nathan Leopold, and ultimately Loeb.

He was about to leave the office to call Randy from the nearest pay phone, when his own phone rang. After he answered, "Dentist," Randy's voice chimed in, "SAYGEE AYGIT?" Will answered "Yaygess," and hung up.

Outside in his pickup Patrick O'Shea was drinking beer and monitoring the office phone calls, nearly falling asleep, when the "SAYGEE AYGIT?" message hit hard right on his suspicious head. He well remembered the consequence of an earlier message he had taped, the "Taygonaygite Taygen," call. Within hours after the call, Hilda had knocked him cold, and the next thing he had been conscious of was a damaged jaw when he awoke several hours later.

"These words can mean only one thing," said Patrick to himself. "Hilda is going to be around, and I'd better get the hell out of here before she blindsides me again. But they aren't done with Patrick O'Shea yet," he mumbled through newly healed jaws. "I might have worked with explosives for the Illinois Highway Department, but by God, I'm going into business for myself now. I'm going to get rid of her and then go on about my life."

Though guilty of the logical fallacy "Post Hoc, Ergo, Proctor Hoc" in attributing the words on the phone to his damaged face, putting the two events together at all and deciding to blow up Hilda the first chance that came around - - - this was as close as Patrick O'Shea had ever come to what John Dewey had termed "Reflective Thinking."

After listening to the news about the skull, Will locked the office and drove to an area Holiday Inn mentioned on the list of businesses that honored AAAA credit cards. The list of eligible firms certainly would not fill up a big book, but just by examining the motels on the list, Will knew he could stay in a different one each night for several weeks, because they were specifically mentioned as places AAAA people recommend.

At the registration desk he said he wanted a room for three nights, smoking or non-smoking and as the clerk was pondering over the unlikelihood that a person without reservations could get the same room three nights in succession, Will handed the clerk his AAAA credit card, not really caring if he could get the same room for three nights or not.

Wherever he stayed, he thought, it would certainly be lonesome. He sorely missed his once friendly office, brimming with happiness and punctuated by laughter when Hilda and Asa were there. But now there was nothing but the memory of matching a dead man's teeth to those on an X-ray. He had to get away until he saw Hilda and Asa again. He knew they were safe, under Randy's wing, but he had had no idea they would be gone this long. Why two weeks?

After the clerk saw the AAAA credit card, his aloof manner suddenly changed. "Yes sir, Mr. Mosley, nice suite on the top floor. Stay as long as you wish, sir." Similar congenial terms flowed from the clerk's mouth as he called the bellhop to make certain the top floor suite was suitably arranged for his special guest with the AAAA credit card.

"They will be a few moments arranging your suite," he told Will. "Our bar is just over here," he pointed. "Have some complimentary drinks before dinner."

Will thanked him, took his room key and headed into the bar, where he relaxed over a drink or two before going up to his room.

The motel room was beautifully arranged with two vases of fresh flowers, a box of chocolates labeled "To Our Special Guest," three touch-tone phones, and a complete list of R and X-rated movies to be shown on TV that evening. Will was impressed, but not enough to get his mind off the skull shown on WGN.

The next morning Will welcomed the pot of coffee outside the door of his room, but he ignored the USA Today newspaper, realizing it would not have much to say about the finding of a skull in Chicago.

In fact, if USA adhered to its guidelines of never printing any article longer than 500 words, they could not even list the names of people around the country who had been murdered on a given evening.

So, he bought a Chicago Tribune, knowing that the Tribune worked closely with WGN, either owning it, or owning the Cubs, whose broadcasts controlled the programming at WGN, or maybe it was the other way around. Maybe WGN owned the Tribune and the Cubs owned WGN. Trying to decide who owned what among the three was, in Will's mind, much like the old children's game, scissors, rocks and paper.

On one of the back pages of the Tribune, Will did find a short item about a skull found near a culvert on Chicago's south side, but nothing was mentioned about glasses, Leopold, or Loeb. Perhaps he had been imagining the entire events of the past few days.

But he knew better than that. It was all real. Too real.

Later that evening, after a few too many Scotches on the Rocks, Will was watching the WGN news on TV when the anchorman announced that Muzafer (Gus) Harrigian, charged with a number of crimes with a high probability of spending the rest of his life in jail, had evidently jumped bail and fled the country at least a week earlier. The announcer said they were just now getting the news because Harrigian had been kept under surveillance, even though not technically under arrest since his trial had begun. And because releasing the news that he was missing would certainly have embarrassed the Chicago Police Department, the police had attempted to keep the matter quiet, hoping to find him any minute. A police spokesperson, according to the announcer, had informed the station that there was really nothing to worry about, because they had issued an APB on Harrigian, which made it almost certain that he would show up.

As an adjunct to the missing Harrigian story, his attorney, Mike Pappas, on behalf of AAAA, Ltd, a completely legitimate organization with investments in banks, hotels, racetracks, gambling associations, airports, and U.S. Treasury Bonds, was offering a $100,000 reward for information leading to the return of Harrigian. "He is innocent of any crime," protested Pappas, "and it is to his advantage to be here because of his very innocence. Just because a person is missing," added Pappas, "is certainly not evidence of any criminal activity on his part. If this were true, the Lindbergh baby would have been suspected of crimes back in the 1930's when he was kidnapped and murdered."

"That's a valid point," Will said to himself. "Not only the Lindbergh baby but also Bobby Franks. He was missing for a while when Leopold and Loeb left his body in the culvert, but nobody suspected Bobby of a crime. Of course, Neither Franks nor the Lindbergh baby had been on trial for several felonies when they turned up missing, but aside from that, it was not a bad analogy Harrigian's lawyer had made. Not bad for a lawyer, at any rate."

The next morning Will scanned the Tribune for news about the disappearance of Muzafer (Gus) Harrigian but found not a word. Perhaps the Tribune was somehow involved with AAAA and was suppressing the news, thought Will, but then again, if WGN carried the story, the Tribune would almost have to mention it also. But it was more likely that the Tribune had already been off the presses when the story broke. He recalled that in Iowa, the Des Moines Register usually was at least a day late with high school football and basketball scores. Why should the Tribune be any different?

Dates on newspapers and magazines no longer served to document the time of events, Will realized. It was possible to purchase a Newsweek or Time, for example, dated August 6 or 7 when the calendar told you it was July 30. To be on top of the news at all, you needed to watch television. He recalled that he had switched from radio to TV as his major source of current news, when growing up in Iowa he had noticed that most of the radio stations, in giving the morning news, did little more than read the morning newspaper to the radio audience.

In his motel room on his final day at the motel, Will called room service for his meals and watched television, searching for more news of either the skull in the culvert or the disappearance of Harrigian. He found no word of either.

The next morning Will checked out of the motel and returned to the shopping center, arriving at his office at about 9:00. He reminded himself to have Hilda get some type of answering machine for the office phone. Perhaps they had called in the past three days. They could have. The news said only that Gus Harrigian was missing, nothing about Hilda or Asa. But then again, someone can be missing, and nobody gives a damn and hardly anyone notices. He knew that had it not been for his checking around with the EPL club and discovering that she was in Memphis, his own wife could have vanished from the planet, without making any real difference. And it would never have been on the TV news or in the newspaper.

With Hilda gone, Will looked over the mail that had come to the office during the past three days. Not much, really. A few bills that he decided not to open, ten or twelve payments from his patients, likewise, and a two-word message on a picture postcard of Wrigley Field. It said "BAYGACK SAYGOON." Seeing the coded message in writing made it more cumbersome to translate than oral messages. At first it looked like the name of a ball player, signed by the Cubs, to turn things around for them in the National League East, where they were now all alone in last place.

As Will was sorting mail and otherwise looking over his office, what he did not see, and small wonder, was a tiny nearly invisible gadget connected to the television, a monitoring device recording what channel he watched and when. This was the work of Patrick, who had entered the office at least three times during Will's absence.

And though the monitoring device was harmless in itself, the dozens of dynamite sticks strategically placed in the panels completely surrounding the room were capable, when triggered, of blowing away half a block of shopping mall.

Patrick had a plan. He knew that sooner or later Hilda would return to the office, possibly along with the old bastard in the wheelchair, and the three of them would be watching Jeopardy or some other ass-hole program at a particular time. Then he would trigger his timer, using all the modern technology he knew, and without endangering himself at all, he could watch the whole place blow up. All he needed to find out was their schedule. He wanted to blow up the place in the evening when not too many people were around, so unless the three had changed their habits radically, they would be sitting around there watching a program, and if he had keyed into the right channel, after two minutes it would be Boom City for all three of the sons of bitches.

Sitting in his pickup, anticipating the explosion, had a strange effect on Patrick. Dwelling on the idea aroused him sexually nearly as much as had been the case in the good old days when he would beat up Hilda at least once a week and then haul her into the bedroom.

But no one would be hauling her into any bedroom when he was finished with her this time. He was certain something was going on between Hilda and someone. Probably with Will, despite his denials, but she could even be making out with that old bastard she wheels around the shopping center. People don't push other people around in wheelchairs unless they are up to something, he decided, downing his second can of Budweiser in the pickup.

Before Patrick was finished with his fantasizing over his clever plan to blast his three enemies off this planet, he noticed that two of them, namely Hilda and Asa, were pulling into the parking lot. Patrick did not want to be seen by Hilda, because he remembered the last time she pulled in with the old guy. But it was too late. Before he could get away the van had pulled up just three parking places away.

After lowering Asa from the van, Hilda walked right past the pickup, but paid no more attention to it than she did to any other vehicle in the lot. From inside the pickup's tinted windows, Patrick noticed that she did not seem to remember his pickup from the other night. "Of course, it was dark then," Patrick told himself. "Besides that, she doesn't know a pickup from a hearse. But where in the hell did she ever learn to slug like that?" he wondered.

"We're back," shouted Hilda, as she wheeled Asa into the dental office. "Anybody home?"

Will was never happier to see two people in his life. If anyone could clear his mind of the awful evening working on the teeth of Randy's corpse, and make him forget the grotesque skull found in a culvert and shown over television, Asa and Hilda could get it done.

"I missed you," said Will. "You're the only family I have. What have you two been up to for the past two weeks?"

"We were just staying with Josephine Harrigian, helping with her new baby, and spending some time with her other kids," said Hilda. "It's a really nice place. You ought to see it some time. Asa, take off your Watchcap and show Will your new look."

Asa complied, removing his Watchcap, along with braids of attached white straggly hair, attached to the inside. Beneath the cap and hair was a nearly full head of white hair, Asa's real hair, neatly groomed and combed straight back in a pompadour fashion.

Will was visibly shaken, upon seeing the new Asa, not so much by his improved appearance, but by the fact he had seen this same Watchcap and partial wig on the corpse delivered to his office by Randy approximately a week before.

"Who gave you the haircut and made a wig under your Watchcap?" asked Asa, knowing what the answer would be.

"Randy. He is a most versatile lad," said Asa. "Barber, tailor, make-up artist. Does a lot of summer theatre work, too. Believe me, I am proud of you and Randy. Perhaps the greatest joy of teaching is to observe the finished product, specifically the students when they approach maturity. You have a wonderful friend there, Will."

"When did Randy do this?" Will asked, fearing the answer. He wondered if this was the very cap worn by the corpse. It had to be.

"Actually," answered Hilda. "He brought in two Watchcaps one day last week, gave Asa a haircut and gave him his choice of hats. We couldn't tell the difference between the two, but Asa pretended to prefer one to the other, took it and put it on. Randy kept the other. Probably threw it away or else used it in his theatre work."

Will was more than somewhat relieved to know the whereabouts of the second Watchcap. It was a small consolation, but he was thankful that Randy had not, when finished with the corpse, removed the wigged cap and given it to Asa. "I've got to quit thinking about this," Will told himself. "Even with Asa and Hilda here, the obsession with the corpse and skull remains." He wondered if he would ever get over the trauma of the dental work on the corpse, and later the shock of seeing the skull on WGN.

"Well, it is certainly great to have you back." Will thought through conversation he could get his mind off the whole thing. "What else did you do when you were gone?"

"You should see the kids' toy room," said Asa. "Wolfgang taught me a Nintendo game that beats that Klondike computer game a thousand ways. And he also taught me how to use the computer for other things, in addition to playing solitaire. Hate to say this but I'm going to miss Wolfgang so much, I'm almost sorry to be back. But not really," he quickly added, hoping not to hurt Will's feelings.

"Did you meet Wolfgang's grandfather?" asked Will, thinking of the missing Muzafer (Gus) Harrigian.

"No," Hilda said, "in fact we didn't see much of Randy after the haircut. Randy, what a guy. If I didn't think so much of Josephine, I could really go for him. That's his wife. He works too hard, though, and when he does have any spare time, he spends it with his community theatre group."

"Not all of it," Will said to himself. And aloud, "What else is new?"

"Well, for one thing," said Hilda, "Asa has a birthday coming up."

"Yes, indeed," Asa added, "First my birthday, then the end of dog days. That's what my mother used to say when we were children in eastern Iowa. The best part of my birthday, to me anyway, was that we were allowed to go swimming a week after. My mother had some strange beliefs about dog days, said if you swam in a river or lake during that time, you would get sick. From July 3 to August 11, often the hottest part of the summer, we had to stay away from the river."

"What are dog days?" asked Hilda.

"Got the name in Ancient Rome. The Romans noticed that in most of July and part of August, Sirius, the Dog Star, rose each morning just ahead of the sun, adding its heat to that of the sun. Really didn't have anything to do with dogs, and there is no evidence that the Earth is affected by heat from Sirius, but I was grown up before I realized it."

"We'll have to have a party to celebrate Asa's birthday," said Hilda. "With a cake and lots of candles."

"They always celebrated our birthdays in the nursing home with cupcakes," said Asa. "No matter how old an individual was, the procedure called for one candle, and a cupcake for everyone, except for the few who were diabetics or otherwise could not ingest sugar."

"What do you want for your birthday, Asa?" asked Will.

"It's a Nintendo game if you can find one. Not the newest model, Randy says no game can be better than Super Mario III, and that is the one Wolfgang taught me. We had a lot of good times together over there. I really am going to miss that lad."

"Which lad?"

"Wolfgang, he was there most all of the time. Being with young people is as close as an old man can come to remaining young. If we do get a Nintendo, Wolfgang said he would come over and hook it up to the TV," said Asa. "He is quite adept at anything electronic. And only eleven years old."

Will thought it might be a first if the three of them wandered into the Toys R US outlet in the mall and convinced them that the Nintendo was for Asa. He wondered how many Super Mario games were purchased by Super Octogenarians. Whatever the cost, it would be worth it to watch Asa play the game.

The three devoted the rest of the day getting the office ready for patients the next day, in addition to interviewing and hiring a dental assistant and receptionist. Perhaps things can get back to normal, thought Will. We can begin paying off our debts, especially the IRS, not too fast to arouse suspicion, but enough to keep them off my back.

He decided to ask Randy how he could best repay the IRS, but then that evening as the three were watching the nine o'clock news, WGN carried a special report that meant Will would probably never get back to normal. The Faustian thoughts returned to haunt him, "Before the first step, you are free. After that, a slave forever."

Chapter 9

THE FUNERAL

As the three of them watched the 9:00 o'clock news that evening, Will was about to resign himself to hearing no news pertaining to his midnight appointment with Randy and the corpse, when a picture of the skull showed on the screen. It was the same shot as previously when a WGN news-tip watcher had found the skull in a south-side culvert. Then the scene shifted as a TV reporter interviewed a Professor from an area dental school, who said, "Although there is not a 100% certainty on identifications from dental X-rays, our files indicate that the teeth in the skull located near the Southside Culvert, match the X-rays of those of Muzafer (Gus) Harrigian."

The reporter explained that Harrigian was currently on trial for several crimes but had been missing for more than a week. He then asked the Professor a follow-up, "Not 100%, but if not 100, what part of 100?"

The Dental Professor answered, "99.44 is as high as we go. We are 99.44% certain the two are one and the same. Dental records have established themselves as identification vehicles, with practically the same certainty as fingerprints."

Back at the studio, while waiting for the hardware commercial and the weather report, the anchorman commented, "Well, it certainly appears that Gus Harrigian is dead, doesn't it?"

"Except for one thing," said the co-anchor.

"What's that?"

"There was a pair of glasses by the skull when they found it. I don't believe Mr. Harrigian wore glasses. I have seen pictures of him."

"Dear God, please, oh please, get rid of this flitter brain working with me," said the anchorman to himself.

And back at the dental office, "Did you know anything about Mr. Harrigian?" Will asked Hilda and Asa, as the three heard the news.

"Nothing at all," said Hilda. Asa shook his head, saying, "Wolfgang is the Harrigian I know best. He is the oldest of the children. This will make it very difficult for him. He mentioned his grandfather on more than one occasion when he was teaching me the Super Mario game."

In Will's mind, the news of the skull's identity, while attesting to his skill in dentistry, also indicated that he himself had willfully assisted in the perpetration of a crime. And if his dental work was good news for Gus Harrigian, wherever he was, it was bad news for himself. If Harrigian got away with this, it would prey on Will's conscience for the rest of his life. And if the police found out what really happened, Will would have the consolation of paying for his crime but would merely be trading a guilty conscience for a life in prison. He wondered which was worse.

Early the next morning Will purchased a Chicago Tribune, and this time the Harrigian story was the lead story on the front page, together with a photograph of Gus Harrigian and a separate shot of his attorney, Mike Pappas.

"This ghoulish event," said Pappas, "completely vindicates my client," but Pappas gave no hint of a libel suit against the media for suggesting that Harrigian had jumped bail and fled the country. When asked about any pending lawsuits, Pappas merely stated, "Anyone who thought Gus Harrigian would jump bail did not truly know the man. It was simply not something he would have done, not his style. Mr. Harrigian was a family man, a good businessman, a staunch Republican, and an honest American. We will not rest until we find who murdered and decapitated him. This type of activity has no place in the great city of Chicago."

That evening, as Will watched the news with Asa and Hilda, the anchorman reported that Attorney Mike Pappas had been granted the court's permission to remove Harrigian's skull from the city morgue, his plea contending that without at least part of the body of the deceased, the pending funeral at Our Lady of Sorrows church would not serve to certify the loss of the loved one to Harrigian's heirs, specifically his bereaved widow Sophia, daughter Josephine, and his five grandchildren, one "an infant who would never experience the joy of seeing her dear departed grandfather."

Will was more than mildly surprised to hear the judge's ruling, bequeathing the skull to the Harrigian family, via the funeral home and the church, but he was well aware that the long powerful tentacles of AAAA, Ltd. reached into the Cook County court system.

But after his initial surprise at the court's ruling, he thought only, "If I have to attend that funeral, I hope to God it's a closed casket affair. I don't ever want to see that dental work again."

With Harrigian's skull lying in state in a closed casket at the Sunset Garden Funeral Parlor, deliveries from florists nearly set an all-time high, according to WGN radio. Will did not catch the names of the closest competitors as recipients of floral arrangements but gathered that they were sent to victims of gang slayings, such as those killed in the 1929 St. Valentine's Day massacre during the height of the Capone era.

But Will thought, as names go, Muzafer (Gus) Harrigian's, like that of Ben Adhem in the poem he had studied in high school, led all the rest. At least "flowerwise," (a term used by the TV people to measure the importance of the funeral). What Will would learn later concerned the funeral of a flower shop entrepreneur named O'Banion, who had been rubbed out by the Capone gang. The ceremony had attracted ten thousand mourners, and the most expensive floral wreath at the funeral had been sent by Al Capone himself.

Will himself had ordered a floral bouquet in the shopping center, using his AAAA credit card to do so, and while not specifying exactly what he wanted, advised them to "make up a nice one and send it to Sunset Gardens." The manager of the mall flower shop was so impressed with the AAAA credit card, that he virtually emptied the contents of the store in tribute to Harrigian.

When Will heard that the flower arrangement was the most elaborate sent to Sunset Gardens, he wished he had either sent nothing, or perhaps only a small bouquet of roses. The last thing he wanted was to run competition with the late Al Capone in sending expensive floral wreaths to murder victims.

It took all of three days for AAAA, Ltd. to arrange for Harrigian's funeral at Our Lady of Sorrows, the popular old lake-front church, utilized in the summer especially, for numerous baptisms, weddings, first communions, confirmations, and of course, funerals. Traditionally, the hotter the weather, the better the business at Our Lady's, because the temperature, with the breeze wafting off Lake Michigan was 15 to 20 degrees cooler than it was a block or two to the west.

"There's more red tape getting a slot in that church calendar than there was in recovering the body of the departed," complained Pappas, in a newspaper interview. Of course, in referring to the body, he meant only part of it, but had Harrigian passed on in an intact body, the funeral would still have been delayed for the same length of time. It was difficult for Father Pius Zybysko to arrange postponements for weddings, having turned over the running of Our Lady of Sorrows to a council elected by parishioners.

The major functions of the church council included arranging for bingo parties, "church warmings" for new parishioners, conducting reading circles, marriage counseling, and inviting guest speakers who discussed "The Joy of Tithing and other Christian Acts." And most of these activities had been planned weeks before anyone had deemed it necessary for Harrigian to be murdered, with only his skull remaining to participate in the ceremony necessary for his pending journey to heaven.

When the day arrived for the funeral, Asa reluctantly remained at the dental office because Our Lady of Sorrows was not handicap accessible, according to Randy. And although Asa was very capable of walking wherever he went, rather than to be pushed in his wheelchair, Randy urged him to stay in the office, promising to send young Wolfgang to see him for Asa's birthday celebration after the funeral ceremonies.

"Wolfgang will need you, now that he has no grandfather," explained Randy. "And of course, the rest of us will need you also. You are part of the family now, especially since my father-in-law is no longer with us."

So as Hilda and Will attended the funeral, Asa remained at their closed dental office, passing the time playing Klondike on the Macintosh, and using the "find" function of the computer to search for words. Asa never tired of typing in "Find Amelia Earhart" or "Find Jimmy Hoffa," after which the computer would fill the screen with a message "Amelia Earhart not found" or "Jimmy Hoffa not found." Asa could amuse himself this way by the hour, while lunching on potato chips and Diet Pepsi.

Our Lady of Sorrows was, as expected, packed for Harrigian's funeral. As Will and Hilda entered the church, expecting to sit together for the ceremony, an usher from AAAA, Inc., after asking them to check their "cameras and any other metallic apparatus," whisked Hilda toward the front of the church, where seated near her were dozens of middle-aged and older women dressed in black. "You will sit with the auxiliary today," the usher whispered to Hilda, as he escorted her to the women. Will's side of the church was male dominated, except for Josephine Harrigian, who sat with Randy and their four sons. Although Will had never previously seen Josephine, he had roughly remembered her from the family pictures Randy had shown him at their class reunion in Iowa City. And Randy had been right when he had told him Josephine was beautiful. Especially after he had used his backstage skill in camouflaging the huge birthmark on one side of her face. Will could not tell which half of her face was real and which was the product of Randy's art.

The ceremony was shorter than some funerals at Our Lady of Sorrows, because Muzafer Harrigian's survivors had asked that there not be a regular Mass, due to the ecumenical nature of the funeral attendants. Father Pius Zybysko read two scripture passages, one on "By their deeds ye shall know them," and the other concerning Lazarus rising from his grave, after which he commended the deceased on his generous acts of charity, pointing out that Harrigian's rise from the grave would be merely symbolic, of course, but nevertheless immortal because of his trust fund for widows and orphans throughout the world. A final passage centered on "My kingdom is not of this world," which reminded Will that even when you die it isn't really the end of the world. Especially if your name happens to be Gus Harrigian and your son-in-law has a good dentist working for him.

No matter how he tried, Will could not remove the traumatic night with Randy and the corpse from his mind. He would be listening to a song (a boys' choir who had recently sung the Star Spangled Banner at nearby Wrigley Field did a beautiful rendition of 'In the Garden'), and when they came to the part, "He walks with me and He talks with me and He tells me I am His own," all Will could think of was the corpse and his matching of the X-rays. Because wherever Will walked, the corpse seemed to be shadowing him, and for Will, a glance at the flower-bedecked casket in front of the altar was more than he could take. He had to look away, for in his mind's eye, all he could see was the grinning skull within, complete with sharpened canines.

As though the hymn "In the Garden" had not exacerbated Will's obsession with the ghoulish skull identified as Harrigian's, Will noticed Randy actually turning around and winking at him, right before a tuxedo-clad barbershop quartet appeared in front of the microphone to sing what was announced as Harrigian's other favorite hymn.

The quartet filled Our Lady of Sorrows church with the trochaic meter of "Dry Bones," including such morbid phrases as "Head bone connected to the neck bone," and then a half-note lower, "Neck bone connected to the collar bone," ditto, "Collar bone connected to the shoulder bone.," etc., to "Hear the word of the Lord."

And while many in the congregation could not keep from snapping their fingers to the rhythm of the refrain, "Dem bones, dem bones, dem dry bones," the spectacle nearly drove Will berserk. In fact, on the line "Dem bones, dem bones gonna walk around," Will had to fight himself to keep from jumping up and screaming, "I did it. I did it!!! I can't stand it anymore!!"

Later, on the way out of the church, with Josephine, Randy, and their four sons lined up (the boys about two years apart in age and looking very much like steppingstones with neckties, if there is such a thing), Will noticed that all four of the boys had inherited the same sharp canines from their grandfather. He supposed that Josephine also had the same type of teeth, but for her this was no time for smiling, so he had no chance for even a cursory dental inspection as he went through the line and out of there as quickly as humanly possible.

Chapter 10

THE REC ROOM

After the funeral, things seemed to be getting back to normal at the office, as Will, Hilda and Asa fell into a comfortable routine. Their days were devoted to getting caught up in their dental practice, with Hilda enjoying her supervisory duties as office manager. And while she made the two new employees comfortable with their work, Ann as receptionist and June as dental assistant, Asa amused himself in his TV-computer room playing computer games, writing his memoirs, and using the "find" function of the computer.

Hilda had done wonders beautifying what they called "Asa's Rec Room," which, for all practical purposes had taken on many aspects of a small apartment, containing a carpeted floor, a refrigerator, a microwave oven, a hot plate, a desk, rolling office chair, three easy chairs, and three World War II Navy footlockers. Asa loved the footlockers, keeping neatly rolled socks, underwear, and pajamas in one, his favorite cereals, cartons of Chesterfields, and cans of sardines in another, and stacks of papers (including his ever-growing pages of memoirs) in the third.

Asa, for his age, was an excellent typist, having learned the skill in Navy Radio School during the war. But it had taken him awhile to adjust to the soft touch of the word processor on the computer, having had a history of resting his fingers on the typewriter keys most of his adult life, which created havoc on the computer screen, filling it with rows and rows of "s's" and "d's," the two keys that had constituted the favorite resting place for his fingers.

And by now, of course, Asa understood that the find function was used to locate a specific word in a text. For example, if Asa was writing his memoirs on the word processor and wanted to add to the part concerning his naval service in World War II, he would press

"Command F," type in "World War" and the computer would immediately go through the text until finding "World War," where it would stop.

But Asa never quit hoping that the computer would have enough brain power to locate something that no one else had ever found. For a diversion this day, he asked the computer to find "Lost Atlantis," to which the computer responded with a brief search and a message, "Lost Atlantis not found." Next, he instructed the computer to find "The Missing Link," but to no avail, as the Macintosh dutifully answered, "The Missing Link not found."

Asa also entertained himself by using the "shut down" function of the Macintosh, for which he was invariably rewarded with a grammatical error, telling him, "You may now switch off your Macintosh safely." In his heart Asa believed that the "may" could someday change itself to the grammatically correct "can," after which the term "safely" might precede the term "switch," bringing the modifiers into what Asa called a "closer harmony."

Hilda was bringing a clean ashtray to Asa, marveling at his skill at the computer, when she noticed that he was writing a letter to Apple Works, notifying them that Macintosh was misspelled on every computer he had seen, and that in honor of John McIntosh, who first cultivated the Apple variety for which the computer was named, they should, at the very least, correct their spelling. From there Asa also mentioned that the "May" should be changed to "Can" in the "switch off" sentence, cautioning Apple Works that inanimate objects cannot technically give permission to a human being.

Meanwhile, Will, with each patient's gaping mouth viewed in his office chair, kept seeing the ghastly mouth of the corpse, held open by Randy on that infamous night two weeks ago. "My God," thought Will, "Has it been only two weeks? So much has happened. Can it ever go back to what it used to be? Before I made that agreement at Greek Island, accepted the locker key at Wrigley Field, and against my better judgment, showed up and waited for Randy and the corpse?"

Although his obsession with the skull hindered his conversation with the dental patients, it had no effect at all on Will's skill as a dentist, and to a very slight degree if a particular patient was suffering from extreme pain or worse, thrashing around in the chair, while flailing fists at him or his new assistant, June, his thoughts would briefly flit from the corpse to the business at hand, because he believed dentists should operate under the same philosophy as actors, "The show must go on."

But alas, even as he ran that bromide through his mind, he could not help but identify stage makeup and inevitably Randy, his partner in crime, with actors and the show that must go on. But Will did manage to finish his workload by five o'clock each evening in time for a welcome Scotch on the rocks in Asa's Rec Room, in company with Hilda and Asa.

They called it their Happy Hour, as Will downed a Scotch or two, while Asa stuck to Diet Pepsi and Hilda sipped what she laughingly called "Paul Mason Chablis," pronouncing the second word the same as the "Mason" in "Mason-Dixon Line," and sounding the "S" on "Chablis," refusing to so much as attempt the standard French pronunciation.

At one time they had watched TV from five until six, beginning with Jeopardy and moving right to the network news, but Hilda soured on Jeopardy, accusing the host Alec of being a pontifical horse's ass, pretending to know everything when he had the answers right in front of him, and showing off whenever he had a chance to say something in French. "You two might like Jeopardy OK," explained Hilda, after two or three glasses of her Paul Mason," but in my opinion it is a horseshit program, probably the most over-rated thing that has ever appeared on television. They even give away cheap prizes."

Asa respected Hilda's opinion, and of course her wish to leave the TV off during Jeopardy, because he, too, had decided to boycott network news until the anchormen quit lying to him.

"Every evening when Dan Rather signs off, he says 'See you tomorrow,' and he has never seen me in my life," explained Asa. "And I will be 86 years old in just a few days. And as for another program I formerly enjoyed, 20/20, I believe it is called, Barbara Walters always ends by saying 'We'll be in touch, so you be in touch.' Doesn't she know it is impossible to be in touch with someone without reciprocation? To think that those TV people get paid for interacting with empty rooms, the very thing I was doing at my old SUI classroom when they shipped me off to the Care Center."

"Tom Brokaw also says he will see us tomorrow, " said Will, pleased at the prospect of getting his mind away from the spurious Harrigian skull, "so let's not watch NBC anymore either."

"Betcher sweet ass," chimed in Hilda, refilling her glass. "TV interferes with talk and that's what people are supposed to do during Happy Hour. Right?

So, we won't watch ABC either. And Asa, we're going to give you a birthday party you'll remember for many years. To your health," she said, raising her glass in a toast.

"Here, here," chimed in Will, fearing his enthusiasm seemed fake as he concentrated on the corpse he had worked on in Chair #3.

So, the three vowed to watch no more television until after dinner when they would take in the nine o'clock news on WGN, after which Hilda would drive to her apartment, while Asa retired to his cot in the X-ray room and Will sacked out on Chair Number 2.

"I think we could get along with only two chairs here," said Will to himself. "Chair #3 has to go."

In the red pickup in the mall parking lot, Patrick had returned to complete the final touches to his demolition project on the dental office. "They are all going to be damned sorry. Just wait and see," he told himself while drinking a can of warm Budweiser.

Patrick had discovered that the three of them, Hilda, plus Will and the old bastard, were in the habit of watching the nine o'clock news on WGN in the evening, just before Hilda took off for wherever she was spending her nights. He considered following her, but ever since she had beaten him nearly to a pulp, he did not want to disrupt his schedule. As it was, his pickup was parked in the mall lot at least three days a week from about 7:00 pm until midnight, and so coincided with the parking schedule of some of the part-time Supermarket employees, that so far as he knew, his pickup truck had not aroused any suspicion.

In the eyes of the shopping center night watchman, the presence of the pickup truck certainly did not merit special attention. He sympathized with the part-time summer employees at the mall, because like himself, most of them were schoolteachers, forced to work at odd jobs during the summer in order to pay their bills and see that their kids got piano lessons and that sort of thing. And two aspects of the red pickup led him to believe the owner was a schoolteacher, somewhere employed in the mall during the summer, possibly as a part-time janitor in Toys R US, definitely not someone planning to blow up a segment of the watchman's beat.

The first hint that the pickup belonged to a schoolteacher, the watchman decided, was the sunshade inside the windshield. While sunshades do not in themselves indicate vehicle ownership by a schoolteacher, the big smiling face on a sunshade was nearly proof positive that the owner was an elementary school teacher. Add to this a recent acquisition of Patrick in the form of an NEA bumper sticker on the rear bumper, and there was no doubt as to his teacher status, the watchman decided, knowing full well that NEA stood for National Education Association.

But in actuality, Patrick O'Shea, when devising his bumper sticker, had no idea that the National Education Association existed. To Patrick NEA meant one thing and one thing only, National Explosives Association. When he decided to leave the Illinois Highway Department to go into business for himself, he placed an advertisement in two or three pulp magazines, in which he was looking for "Chapter Sponsors" to "Keep America Free by Keeping Neighborhoods American." A stack of well-placed dynamite could get undesirable neighbors out of the neighborhood a hell of a lot faster than a burnt cross, reasoned Patrick.

And he was correct in anticipating interest in NEA among the readers of the pulp magazines, for in less than a week more than two dozen responses to his ad showed up in his Post Office Box, each one containing a check, cash, or money order for the $25 membership fee.

In fact, since a total of five charter memberships had been mailed from Dubuque, Iowa, he considered the Mississippi river community as a potential flagship chapter, to be followed by three other Iowa towns, each of which had provided two charter members. These were Ottumwa, Waterloo and Fort Dodge.

His new NEA business kept him too busy to devote 100% of his thoughts to blowing up Will's office, but he had reached a point where it was as good as done. The tiny TV monitor he had planted, indicated that the only channel they watched was WGN, which was Channel 9 on regular television, Channel 10 on cable direct. He had ascertained that Will's office TV was not connected to any cable, so all Patrick had to do was attach a timing device, geared to go off at a specific time when the TV was turned on and tuned to WGN.

He decided to sneak into the office that evening, since the three were in the habit of leaving the office vacant for at least two hours when they went out for dinner. Then he would rig his timer to Will's television, quietly leave the parking lot, take a brief organizing trip across Iowa, with stops at Dubuque, Waterloo, Fort Dodge, and Ottumwa, and when he returned to the mall after his itinerary, he would have the fun of seeing what that dental office looked like after it had blown to hell, taking all three of the bastards with it.

"They deserve to die," muttered Patrick, after he had sneaked into the office, and set his timer. As he left the mall area in search of a tavern that played a lot of Country Western music, he thought, "Maybe those three go together, Hilda, Will and the old man. But three other things that go together are beer, Country Western music and dynamite." He was smiling at his poetic discovery as he squealed out onto the highway. "What a great song that would be," he said to himself, "Beer, Country Western, and Dynamite. Now, exactly where in the hell is Dubuque?"

The next morning Asa awakened, happy as a seven-year-old, realizing it was his birthday. "August 6 again," he announced to Will, over their ritual cup of instant coffee. "Think of that. 86 on August 6. And I remember most of them."

"Which birthdays are the most vivid to you," asked Will, unsuccessfully trying to shake the memory of the skull from his mind.

"Well, for starters, 1945 was most memorable. That was the day we dropped the atom bomb on Hiroshima. And on this date in 1941 the Allies began their invasion of North Africa, with hundreds of soldiers killed. And in 1890 on this date, some years before I was born, we had our first electrocution in the United States. Auburn, New York, I believe. The culprit was a convicted axe-murderer named William Kemmler. Thomas Edison supplied the electrical equipment for the ceremony. The execution took eight minutes before Kemmler stopped squirming and thrashing around in the chair."

Will was sorry he had asked, for each of Asa's recollections was as morbid as his own memory of that horrendous night working on the corpse in Chair #3. And although he could occasionally go as long as two or three minutes without the skull coming back to haunt him, that could hardly be classified as much of a respite.

"Happy birthday, happy birthday," sang Hilda, entering the front door. "For breakfast here are cupcakes and champagne. I'll bet you didn't get that at hot lunch when you were teaching school, right Asa?"

"Right!" said Asa, as the phone rang.

After answering the phone Will told Asa and Hilda there would be two guests at their Happy Hour after work. "Wolfgang and Max," he said.

"Great lads," said Asa. "Max is made of the same stuff as Wolfgang, though a bit younger. Good boys, both of them."

"Do either of you know who named those kids?" Will asked.

"Well," said Hilda, "Josephine talked to me a lot about the children. They are her whole life, with Randy gone most of the time. She said they named the oldest boy Wolfgang because in the hospital the day after the baby was born, Randy took one look at him and said, "He looks like he ought to be called Wolfgang."

"How about Max?" Asked Will.

"Josephine explained that. It brought tears to my eyes. Right before their second baby was born, Josephine was depressed because of the unsightly birthmark on one side of her face. She feared that Randy would leave her, because a lot of people do that sort of thing. But instead of that, Randy used his theater skills and made Josephine up, fixing her face with makeup so no one could tell the difference. It was wonderful."

"But how did Max get his name," repeated Will.

"Oh, I forgot to mention that. He was named Max Factor Harrigian, after the firm where Will purchases makeup for his community theatre work. Randy is just wonderful with makeup. Made himself up one night to look like Barbara Bush. It was a scream."

"Yes, he's very good," agreed Will, again obsessed with the horrible memories of the night when Patrick dressed up to look like Hilda, pushing a corpse, made up to resemble Asa.

The patients soon started arriving and Hilda told Asa they would begin celebrating his birthday for real when Wolfgang and Max got there at five.

As usual Asa was happily biding his time by drinking Diet Pepsi, chain- smoking Chesterfields, playing computer games in the rec room, completing a chapter of his memoirs and exploring new items for the Macintosh to locate with its find function. "Find the Loch Ness Monster," commanded Asa, to which the computer replied, "The Loch Ness Monster not found." This was followed by, "Find an honest man for Diogenes," after which came the predictable reply, "An honest man for Diogenes not found."

"This computer isn't any smarter than I am," chuckled Asa, as he resumed his work on his memoirs.

At five o'clock, Randy's combination nanny-chauffeur-body guard, employed for the sole purpose of protecting his sons when they traveled anywhere, parked a van at the east end of the supermarket parking lot, and told Wolfgang and Max to ride their bicycles over to the dental office, as though they were two patients, and to remain there no later than 7:00 p.m., when he would have the van in front of Will's office and take them home.

After locking their bicycles in front of the office, the boys came in, carrying a package and shouting, "Happy birthday, Asa."

"You'll never guess what this is," they told Asa, as Hilda took them into the Rec Room where he was asking the computer to "Find the name of the unknown soldier," but to no avail. "Someday, someday, if I keep asking this Macintosh to find something no one else has ever found, I will be rich and famous," said Asa, as he thanked the boys for remembering his birthday.

Hilda had purchased Asa's favorite kind of cake, chocolate with white frosting, and had placed a total of 14 candles on it, eight of these were in a circle on one side of the rectangular cake, the other six on the other side. For the event she had purchased a new card table at the nearby K-mart, had covered it with a birthday tablecloth, and had placed five birthday paper plates and birthday paper cups around the table. Asa, Hilda, and Will each had an entire side of the card table to themselves, while Wolfgang and Max shared the fourth side.

As she was lighting the candles, Max commented, "only 14 candles? Asa is a lot older than 14."

Wolfgang, raising his eyebrows while rolling his eyes, explained to Max. "The first eight candles are for ten years each, meaning eighty. The other six are for one year apiece. Asa is 86. OK?"

"Yes," said Asa, "86 on the 6th."

"Well," said Max, "In June Wolfgang was 11 on the 9th and I was 9 on the 11th. But we didn't know you then, but happy birthday any way. Now can we give you your present?"

"Right after our happy birthday song," promised Hilda, as Asa, with Hilda's assistance blew out the candles in no more than three breaths.

Then came the "Happy birthday to Asa" song, after which they had cake, with Asa's favorite ice cream (French vanilla) on top.

Will and Hilda presented Asa with a key to a golf cart, explaining that it was in the X-ray room, and would take the place of his wheelchair if he liked it. Also, they presented him with a lap computer he could use when seated in the golf cart or anywhere else he happened to be.

Asa was certainly most appreciative, but what really brought tears to his eyes were the two presents from Wolfgang and Max, namely a Nintendo Entertainment System and a disk labeled "Super Mario Bros. 3." On the package was the comment, "The biggest, most exciting Mario Bros. adventure yet!"

"Strange syntax," said Asa, reading the words aloud, "but the best game I have ever seen in my life and I'm 85."

"Eighty-Six," corrected Hilda, as Will sat there, struggling to look interested and pleasant, but unable to free his mind from the sight of the corpse brought to his office at least ten days before, pushed into his office in Asa's wheelchair, and by the very father of these two great kids. "Must get their decency from their mother," he said to himself, while at the same time feeling more than a twinge of guilt for his negative thoughts about Randy, who despite his criminal activities and black humor, was the best friend he had ever had.

"How do we make it work?" asked Asa. "I have missed Mario since I left you lads. And of course, I missed you, too."

"I'm sure the people at Toys R Us would have someone who could hook it up," said Hilda. "I think they are still open."

"We can hook it up for you, Asa," said Max, looking at Wolfgang. "Can't we?"

"Sure, if you want me to," said Wolfgang, looking at the three adults as though to be granted permission.

"Are there instructions in the package," asked Will. "Maybe I could help."

"We don't really need them," responded Wolfgang. "Do you have a VCR?"

"No but we can get one," said Will. "I'd like to see how it works."

"You don't need a VCR to run Mario and Luigi," said Wolfgang. And within seconds he was kneeling on the floor in front of the TV, hooking up the Nintendo, complete with hand controls, after which he inserted the disk, turned on the TV and switched it to channel 3.

Two more little clicks of the hand controls and Mario was on the screen dancing back and forth and stomping on enemies, in sort of a demonstration scene.

"Here you are, Asa," said Wolfgang. "Want to show them what you can do?"

Asa pulled his chair up in front of the TV screen, held the control in his hands and prepared to start the game.

"What's the object?" asked Hilda, as Asa fidgeted in his chair, anxious to get started with the game.

"To take Mario or Luigi (if you are playing with two players) through as many lands or worlds as you can before they get killed," said Wolfgang. "You can read about it in the little pamphlet in the package."

"And if Mario does get killed four times, you can push 'continue' and get four more lives," added Max.

"Well, I'll be," said Hilda.

Hilda and Will watched Asa, as he began to maneuver Mario through Level One of Grass Land, and no sooner had Mario stomped on two goombas and a para-goomba before Hilda started to laugh.

Will wasn't laughing, though he was interested and more than fascinated by Asa's hand-eye coordination. He wondered how many 86-year-olds had received Nintendo games for their birthdays.

"He looks just like Donahue," laughed Hilda.

"I do?" asked Asa, pushing the pause function, which he had learned to do by observation when he was staying with the boys before the funeral.

"No, Mario does. When he jumps up and stomps on that crawly dumb-looking thing and then hops over to stomp on another, he is acting just like Donahue when he hops from one person in the audience to another with that stupid microphone in his hand."

"Mario doesn't have a microphone," said Max, who had never heard of Donahue, "but after you play a few times you can get Mario a raccoon tail, or a frog suit, and he can get fire power or Hammer-Brothers power too. Also, a Tanooki suit."

"No shit," said Hilda, covering her mouth as soon as the words escaped her.

She need not have worried, for neither Wolfgang nor Max acted as though they had heard her scatological remark. And Asa was so busy struggling through Level I that he was completely impervious to any remark when the control boards were in his hands.

"Here, Will," said Asa, after working his way through Levels I and II, "Try it. The controls are quite elementary, I assure you. Press the 'A' button to jump, the 'B' button to go faster, and with your left hand, push up to go up, to the right to move right, left to left, and down to either duck or go down. At times you will wish to duck, in order to avoid bullets that occasionally fly through the air attempting to kill Mario."

"You're exactly right, Asa," said Wolfgang, knowing Asa was merely repeating to Will what Wolfgang had taught Asa a week or so earlier. "I wish I had a teacher like you instead of the ones I have."

"Me too," agreed Max.

Will's first attempt with Mario was a near nightmare, as he entered what Wolfgang called "Boom-Boom's Fortress," for no sooner had he started through the fortress when Mario was crushed by what the boys called a "Thwomp," a pile-driving stone block, that landed on Mario, reducing his lives from four to three.

"Try it again," said Asa. "It takes a while, "he added, knowingly.

Will managed to get through the thwomps and leap across fiery chasms on his third try, when he confronted a ghastly-looking enemy, appearing very much to be a walking skeleton.

"What's that?"

Wolfgang pushed the pause button and explained, "That's Dry Bones. If Mario jumps on his back, Dry Bones will die, but only for a few seconds. Then he comes back to life. Mario can't kill Dry Bones. It tells about it in your pamphlet."

For a moment Will thought this was another of Randy's practical jokes, as his mind returned to the funeral when Randy turned around and smiled at him just before the trio sang, "Dem bones, dem bones, gonna walk around, dem bones, dem bones, gonna walk around."

Because that was exactly what they were doing. And if you got rid of them for a moment, they were as sure to return as his memory of that awful night fixing the corpse's teeth. And again, a few days later, seeing the skull shown on Channel Nine.

"You take it, will you?" asked Will. "I'll watch. How often does this Dry Bones thing come after Mario?"

"Only once in each world. In the fortress," explained Max, looking at Wolfgang to see if he had it right.

For the next hour the three adults experimented with Super Mario III, with Hilda and Will improving fast, as they caught on to the basic moves as commanded by the controllers, with Asa, enjoying his role as a relative Mario expert, advising them as they progressed. Wolfgang and Max stood by, helping only when asked.

"Before you boys have to go," said Asa, "tell me again how many enemies Mario has in this game?"

"If you count small differences, like green koopas and red koopas, and green and red paratroopas, Mario and Luigi have 66 enemies." said Wolfgang. "We can bring over our book next time if you want to know all their names. Or we can name them now, but you'd be better off to learn the game. We have to leave anyway. It was a great party. Thanks. It was great to meet you, Uncle Will."

"Happy birthday again, Asa," added Max. "And thanks for letting us come over, Aunt Hilda. Goodbye, Uncle Will."

All three adults had tears in their eyes when the boys left at exactly seven o'clock.

"Think of that," Asa said, as the three adults resumed the game. "Those lads can name 66 imaginary creatures in a game and there probably are not ten grammar school students in the county who can name the 50 states."

"Grammar school, my ass," said Hilda. "I can't name the 50 states."

Ignoring her language, which appeared to be getting more salty these days, in Asa's opinion, he added. "And they can tell you the difference between a Koopa Troopa, a Koopa Paratroopa, and a Gargantua Koopa Troopa, in two colors, but they would be hard pressed to explain the difference between an adverb and an adjective. To say nothing of the difference between a nominative absolute and an adjunct accusative."

"Let's get on with the game," suggested Will.

For the next hour the three resumed the Super Mario III game, in the form of a tournament, where Asa drew a bye in the semi-final or first round, as Hilda and Will fought it out to determine who would reach the finals with Asa. Will won the game, Hilda went out for pizza, and Asa thoroughly trounced Will in the final round, reaching level 6 of the Grass World.

After downing the pizza and enjoying another piece of birthday cake, washed down with Diet Pepsi, Asa defeated Hilda, as Will sat out, surprising both of them by acquiring what the boys called a warp whistle to take him all the way to World IV or the Land of Giants.

During the final game of the evening, Will noticed that if he stayed away from the fortress and looked the other way when someone else was visiting the habitat of the Dry Bones, his mind stayed completely free of the night of the corpse in the wheelchair.

At ten o'clock Hilda said, "I'd better be leaving. What do we do tomorrow?" she asked Will.

"A little remodeling, if it's OK with you. I'm getting rid of Chair #3, putting up a little partition there, and moving in a roll-a-way. Also," he said, "I've got a new X-ray machine coming in. Too many problems with this one when you were gone."

Asa said, apologetically, "Sorry I made you miss the WGN news. But I was so engrossed in Mario, I forgot what time it was."

"That's fine," said Will. "Me, too."

"Yah, who gives a shit about the news," said Hilda. "See you tomorrow."

After they left, Asa fell asleep on the couch while Will played the Nintendo game for two more hours, neither realizing that the walls surrounding them were insulated with enough dynamite to blow them far beyond World Eight, the end and ultimate goal of Super Mario III.

All Will needed to do to bring Nagasaki and Hiroshima to his office was to tune in the TV to Channel 9 between nine and eleven p.m.

Chapter 11

The Inspector

At approximately 3:00 p.m. on the following Tuesday, Inspector Walter O'Kowski walked into Will's office, with a pained look in his eyes and his right hand holding his jaw. After explaining to the receptionist that he had no appointment but happened to be in the neighborhood, he was asked to have a seat in the reception room and told that Doctor Mosley would work him in between patients as soon as possible.

Inspector O'Kowski was a third-generation Chicago area policeman, having been preceded by his father Michael "Mickey" O'Kowski, and before that by his immigrant grandfather, Vladimir O'Kowski. When grandfather Vladimir had arrived at Ellis Island shortly after the turn of the century, an immigration official named Jimmy Duggan had inadvertently misspelled Vladimir's last name, which he had given correctly as Okowski, but which Duggan had changed to O'Kowski, saying, as he handed him his papers, "Sure and begorra, it's a great country we are having," to which Vladimir had responded, "Da."

Moving to the south side of Chicago, Vladimir worked three weeks in a meat packing plant before applying for a position on the fire department. Through a mis-shuffling of his application papers, they landed on top of the desk of Police Chief Paddy Maginnis, who hired Vladimir without so much as an interview, knowing full well that when it comes to good hard-working policemen, a true son of the old sod (which he believed O'Kowski to be) could never be matched.

Thirty years later Mickey followed in his father's footsteps, diligently performing the duties of a Chicago policeman during the Capone era, and now Walter himself, sitting in the office nursing a bad tooth, was but a few years short of getting a pension, the true goal of every red-blooded policeman he had ever known.

At 3:30 O'Kowski was ushered to chair #1, one of only two chairs in Will's hastily remodeled office.

"What's the problem?" asked Will.

"Hell of a toothache," responded O'Kowski. "That's problem number one. And when we take care of that I'd like to ask you just a few things about problem number two."

"Let's take a look," said Will, as O'Kowski seated himself in the chair.

"Yes, yes indeed, it could be abscessed," Will continued, "Can't work on an abscessed tooth. How long has it been bothering you?"

"About as long as problem number two," said O'Kowski, trying to muster up a grin.

A slight shiver rippled through Will's body at the repeated words, "problem number two." When your conscience bothers you, thought Will, you believe everyone knows your deepest secrets, but maybe I'm a little too jumpy, he decided.

Will handed him four sample packages of penicillin, telling him to take one every four hours until all were used, and to come back or see another dentist in ten days. He also gave O'Kowski two sample packs of pain killers, directing him to take one now and every twelve hours after that as needed.

"I figured you'd have a dozen assistants in here," said O'Kowski, "and here you are practically all by yourself. I'm Inspector Walter O'Kowski from the Chicago police."

"Nice to meet you, Inspector," Will said, amazingly unalarmed, because knowing Randy Harrigian's sick sense of humor and penchant for practical jokes, he figured his old high school buddy was behind this.

"I would have had this tooth fixed three or four days ago," O'Kowski said, "but those assholes downtown told me to save it for you."

"That's a good one," said Will, wondering if the alleged O'Kowski would have dared call Randy an asshole to his face, adding, "but you really should take care of your teeth as soon as possible. The longer you wait, the worse it will get. Why did you, 'save it for me' way out here in the boondocks? It must have been painful for you. How much are you getting paid to carry that toothache around?" Will added, somewhat enjoying the joke.

"Look, Doc, I didn't come here to answer questions, but to ask them," said O'Kowski, gruffly. "But you ask, 'why me?' So, I'll tell you. I'll answer your questions if you answer mine."

"Sounds fair to me," said Will, looking over his patient, thoroughly convinced now that he had been sent by Randy.

"Well, here's why I'm here. There is so much crime these days and our police force has grown so much, that if a car dealer is suspected of homicide, we send a cop who needs a car. If a real-estate developer turns out to be crooked, we will send someone to see him who wants to buy a house. We had an eye-ear-nose and throat doctor involved in an ax-murder case last week and they sent an inspector with strep throat to see him. It worked, too. Nailed the son of a bitch."

"What if the suspect happens to be an undertaker?" asked Will, enjoying Randy's game, "Do you send a dead cop from downtown to interview him?"

"We're working on that," said O'Kowski, grimly.

"Are you a tax man?" asked Will, smiling. "I've had a problem with the IRS, but the person who sent you (thinking it was Randy) knows we are getting it taken care of."

"No, homicide, but think nothing of it," said O'Kowski. "The fact is that your name came up for sending $2000 worth of flowers to Gus Harrigian for his funeral. Downtown, they think the person who sent the most flowers probably killed the son of a bitch. Personally, I'm happy Harrigian was murdered, and just by talking to you I know you didn't have a thing to do with it. Just tell me why you sent so damned many flowers to the dirty bastard, and I'll be on my way."

At once, Will saw the extent of Randy's joke. He probably had notified the two florists who honored AAAA credit cards, telling them to shoot the works with the floral arrangement at his father-in-law's funeral. Randy's mind worked in strange ways, thought Will, and he would go to any extent to pull off a joke, including having "Dry Bones" played at the funeral after planting the skull and glasses in the same general spot where Leopold and Loeb murdered Bobbie Franks.

"Well, it was a mistake, sort of. A misunderstanding," said Will. "The guy who handled the order got the decimal point in the wrong place or something. I figured Harrigian was worth only $20, so it was only natural for the clerk to misunderstand. Now, Mr. O'Kowski, why don't you go back and tell your bosses 'downtown' that you ran into a real tough cookie here, and that I caught on to your bullshit right away."

"Did you get billed yet?" O'Kowski seemed to be ignoring Will's last comment.

"Billed for what?" asked Will.

"The flowers, for Christ's sake."

"I don't know," Will answered. "My office manager takes care of the funds. But tell me, what if I had sent $10,000 worth of flowers, would that prove I killed Harrigian?"

"Not in itself," O'Kowski conceded, getting out of the chair. "But there is one more thing I need to clear up."

"What's that?"

"OK, watch carefully," O'Kowski said, moving to directly before a framed certificate on the wall about 20 feet from Will. "What is this stuff on the certificate?"

Will said, looking at the certificate on the wall, "Illinois Pedodontic Association. I'm a member."

"Wondered what the hell that word in the middle was," said O'Kowski. "I notice you can read this from 20 feet away. That means 20-20 vision, right? Or are you wearing contacts?"

"No, my eyes are OK. Always have been 20-20."

"One more thing," said O'Kowski.

"Yes?"

"Where are your glasses?"

"I don't wear glasses. I just said, I don't need any corrective lenses. Never wore glasses, never will." Will wondered what the punch line in Randy's theatrical scene would be.

"But," said O'Kowski, whirling around toward Will, and pointing his finger at him, "if you did wear glasses, they would be plain window glass, right?"

"I suppose so," conceded Will, "and if I wore a hearing aid, it would not contain an amplifying device."

"I don't give a shit about hearing aids. The reason I'm here has to do with those glasses found by Harrigian's skull. Whoever murdered

Harrigian left his glasses at the scene, and they turned out to be nothing but plain window glass. The exact kind you would wear if you didn't need any. The people at Chicago homicide say that automatically rules out everyone who wears corrective lenses of any type, which is approximately two million people. And of the five subjects who blew at least $1000 in flowers for Harrigian's funeral, you and you alone are the only one who does not need glasses."

O'Kowski paused briefly, for dramatic effect and added, "But it could be coincidence. You're not going anywhere are you, Doc? I'll have to tell you that if you leave the area, it's hard to tell what those horses' asses downtown will suspect you of. As for me, I'm satisfied with your explanation. Just want to look around a bit to clear everything up."

"Go ahead," said Will, laughing and pointing to the Rec Room. "You can help yourself to coffee or whatever."

Before calling in his next patient, Will enjoyed a good silent chuckle, wondering what outrageous prank Randy would come up with next. It made him feel better about that horrible night with the corpse, just to know that Randy was making enough of a joke about it to send that actor O'Kowski out to razz him about the whole thing. Only someone with a drama background in community theatre could have written lines as stupid and illogical as were tossed around by O'Kowski. By god, it was funny, when you thought about it. He was going to quit worrying about the whole thing.

As Inspector O'Kowski walked into the Rec Room, Asa was busy writing his memoirs on the computer, so involved in his World War II Navy service that he was practically reliving the past. One nice thing about writing memoirs, decided Asa, was that if you really got into typing a record of events that took place 50 years ago, it was as close as one could possibly come to discovering the Fountain of Youth. The chapter Asa was working on had to do with Boot Camp at the Great Lakes Naval Training Station. At that time, he was 35 years old, nearly a generation older than many of the recruits, but young, very young, by his present standards.

Involved as he was in the typing of his memoirs, Asa could hardly be blamed for failing to notice the presence of O'Kowski in the room.

"I'm inspector O'Kowski," said Walter, after which Asa, caught in his World War II warp zone, jumped to his feet, whirled, saluted, and said "Company 320, ready for your inspection, sir."

"No, not that kind of inspector," said O'Kowski, impressed with the agility of the senile fart at the computer. "I'm an inspector with the Chicago police department."

"My name is Smitherman," responded Asa, as he resumed his seat at the computer. "What would you like to inspect? My possessions are neatly arranged in the footlockers," he added, pointing to the footlockers by the wall.

"No, Chicago inspectors do not inspect, they investigate," said O'Kowski, slurping from a cup of instant coffee.

"Investigate?"

"Yes, everyone in the department investigates. I investigate myself."

"You investigate yourself?" responded Asa, trying to picture the introspective effort involved in such an activity. "Is that reflexive or intensifying? Have you ever found yourself to be guilty?"

"Don't give me any of that happy flexatensifying horseshit," said O'Kowski, slightly irritated at the old man's irreverence. "Who the hell are you talking to?"

"Whom," corrected Asa.

"Forget it, Old Man. What the hell are you making there? I never got into computers," O'Kowski admitted, looking over Asa's shoulder at the Macintosh, "thought when they came out, I was too old to learn something new. But you're sure as hell older than I am, aren't you?"

"Which question do you want answered first?" Asked Asa. "I have plenty of time if you do. I'm retired, you know."

"Bullshit," responded O'Kowski, as he left, but not before he had planted a bug behind the television set, to overhear any conversation in the room that might serve to implicate the bastard dentist. "I'm getting out of here."

A glance at his watch told O'Kowski that it was 4:55, giving him only five minutes to get to his car before the office closed, with the prospect of implicating conversation sent to his receiver from the concealed microphone behind the TV.

At five o'clock, as was their recent custom since resolving to boycott the Jeopardy program, Will, Asa, and Hilda spent a few minutes with their own version of Jeopardy, coming up with answers, to which the other two would guess the question.

Will began, while sipping a Scotch, "Next answer, 9-W."

"What is an airplane," guessed Hilda.

"No," said Will.

"What is the second syllable of your eyetooth, followed by the first letter of an unnecessary tooth?" said Asa.

"Close," said Will, thinking of canine and wisdom, "but you're both wrong. The correct question is 'Do you spell your last name with a V, Herr Weber?'"

"Ugh," said Hilda. "My turn. The answer is Bobbie Franks."

Will shuddered, wondering how Hilda knew about Bobbie Frank, as well as Leopold and Loeb, but then recalled their conversation on their earlier trip to Memphis. He marveled at her memory.

"Who was killed by Leopold and Loeb?" volunteered Asa.

"Wrong," said Hilda.

"I give up," said Will, wondering what the answer would be.

"The correct question is, "What was the name of your brother who was murdered in 1968, Teddy?"

"I don't get it," said Will.

"I do," said Asa. "A chap named Franks is asking Teddy Kennedy the name of his brother. So, Teddy responds 'Bobbie, comma, Franks.' Superb, Hilda. Most superb."

"Thanks," said Hilda. "Your turn, Asa,"

"I have two, then let's play Nintendo," said Asa.

"Number one, Chicago Overcoat."

Hilda and Will gave up, after which Asa explained, "What is the Chicago underworld's term for a coffin?"

"Morbid," said Hilda.

"Number two, Chicago Amnesia."

"That's easy," said Will. "What is the term for forgetfulness on the part of Chicago eyewitnesses to crimes?"

Had Inspector O'Kowski been in his car to hear the Jeopardy-game part of the conversation, he would have become suspicious of the activities in the bugged Rec Room, but because he had forgotten where he had parked his car in the huge lot, he was a few minutes late in arriving.

At the same time O'Kowski turned up the volume on his receiver in his Police Buick, Randy bounced into the Rec Room, disguised as Mario in the Nintendo game, complete with a brick layer's hat, blue overalls, red shirt, mustache and oversized nose. It was the first time Will had seen him since Muzafer Harrigian's funeral, and then not to talk to. Will had a lot of questions to ask, if he could get Asa and Hilda away for a few minutes.

"OK," said Randy, turning the TV set on to the partially completed Mario 3 game, "you said you wanted lots of lives for Mario, right? Well, the two boys could do it better, but they're on their way back from camp today. So, I thought I'd give it a shot."

"The important issue is," said Asa, as O'Kowski listened in his car. "Mario and Luigi are about to get killed by Boss Bass. He kills everything that crosses his path. Boss Bass protects his territory."

"I know," said Randy as he turned down the sound and used the Nintendo controller to maneuver Mario beyond the clutches of Boss Bass. "What you do, if you don't want Boss Bass to kill Mario or Luigi, is give them fire power. Then they can kill Boss Bass and get that obstacle out of the way."

Dead silence followed in the Rec Room as the trio of novices watched Randy take Mario to Level 4, where he succeeded in obtaining 99 lives for him. Then he did the same for Luigi.

"I'm going to learn to do that," promised Asa. "All it takes is patience, fortitude, and good timing. At least that's what your boys told me."

Overhearing the conversation in the car was almost too much for O'Kowski. "Who the hell is this Boss Bass?" he asked himself. "And who in Christ's name are Mario and Luigi? This is more than I expected. How the hell big is this dentist's gang anyway? The way they are talking about mass murder makes Al Capone look like a god-damned altar boy."

Hilda, realizing that Randy might wish to speak privately with his old school chum, arranged with Asa to ride double in the golf-cart to the other end of the mall for gyros sandwiches and antipasto. As she was leaving, she asked Randy, "You'll be eating with us won't you?"

"I'd like to, but thanks, I've got too much to do. I have to call the boys and a couple of other things," said Randy.

After Hilda and Asa left, Will smiled at Randy, saying "That Inspector O'Kowski you sent out here was funny as hell, but honest to God, I'd like to forget this ever happened."

In the car O'Kowski listened carefully, especially about the "Inspector O'Kowski you sent out here" part, which made him suspect that his supervisor, Commissioner Callahan, was on the take. Rusty Callahan was the bastard who had given him the assignment. It wouldn't be the first time that high ups on the force had involved themselves with the mob. "That dirty son of a bitch," said O'Kowski, vowing to pull the rug out from under the whole department before he was through.

O'Kowski waited for Callahan's voice, which he would recognize as soon as he responded to the dentist's "I'd like to forget this ever happened."

But inside the Rec Room, Randy, seeing that Will was honestly upset at what he had perceived as some type of practical joke, put his finger to his lips in the established "shh" position and whispered, "Let's talk about it, but we had better have Mario and Luigi listen in, too," as he turned the sound up nearly full blast on the Nintendo game, now resting between Levels 4 and 5 of the Water World.

"Aha," muttered O'Kowski in his Police Buick. "I know it's Callahan. He drinks so much in the afternoon, it wrecks his vocal cords by this time of day. So, his voice sounds like a loud wheezy bad-smelling whisper."

In the conversation that followed, with the two friends facing each other and standing less than a foot apart, Randy convinced Will that he had nothing to do with Inspector O'Kowski's visit earlier that day, and that even though Will thought their reasoning on the window-glass lenses was hilarious, it was no more than you could expect from the Chicago police force.

As for the expensive floral wreath purchased with Will's AAAA credit card, more than one business that honored AAAA cards did so out of fear, considering their cooperation with AAAA as a form of insurance against vandalism or even worse, murder. Perhaps Will shouldn't use that AAAA card for a while. He didn't actually need to use it, Randy explained, with Hilda now having access to an account containing more than $300,000.

"Christ, I really am worried now," said Will to himself, as Randy departed. He turned down the sound on Super Mario III, poured himself another Scotch and awaited the return of Asa and Hilda. He was not hungry.

Meanwhile, in the Police Buick, wondering what caused the hellish music from the Rec Room, but deciding he had heard enough to suspect Callahan, Inspector O'Kowski left the area for the rest of the evening, not quite believing what he had overheard.

After returning with the lunch, Hilda and Asa remained with Will until after ten o'clock, happily involved in playing Super Mario 3, until Hilda said, "My God, it's almost 10:30. Time for me to go home. And Will, don't you dare practice when I'm gone. You're getting too good too fast. Don't shut Mario off though, because as Wolfgang said, it will kill him for good and put us clear back into World I."

Will had noticed that when he was engrossed with the Mario game, his worries escaped his mind, at least for a while. This was true with the new worry about O'Kowski, as well as the old ones about the corpse, the skull, and the dry bones song at the funeral. He did not even notice this evening, that he had again failed to watch the WGN news.

As he lay down in Chair #2, trying to sleep, with his conscience nagging at him, while wondering what to do next, he recalled a western story he had read in a pulp magazine when he was about 12 or 13 years old. The hero of the story was a lone cowboy who had shot and killed another cowboy by accident. The memory of the deed tormented him, until one day when he deliberately shot a man who had pulled a gun on him. After that he no longer worried about the early accidental killing, but his conscience bothered him about the shooting in self-defense. That is, until later, when he had an argument with his best friend, and shot and killed him.

The point was that each deed, while worse than the previous deed, served the purpose of clearing his conscience of all previous deeds. The final paragraph in the cowboy story showed the cowboy, pistol in hand, slowly riding on his horse to the home of his mother. The important thought left with Will by the cowboy story was the cowboy's belief that by killing his own mother, he would forget his other crimes and would be able to sleep better.

"In other words," thought Will, "by applying this to my own life, I can forget about the corpse and the skull only by doing something worse. If I kill someone, perhaps Inspector O'Kowski, the corpse and skull will never cause another sleepless night."

Chapter 12
THE EXPLOSION

Two days later, while returning to the Chicago area in his "just like new" Ford, Patrick O'Shea was marveling at the recent turn of events in his life. Almost overnight his life had changed from being a nobody working for bureaucratic bastards on the Illinois Highway Department, to becoming a real leader, complete with those three elements often accompanying those fortunate individuals who hit it big in private enterprise, namely power, money, and status.

Before leaving for his Iowa itinerary to organize chapters in the NEA, Patrick had stopped at the post office, which was overflowing with membership applications, and much more importantly, with membership fees, in the form of money orders, certified checks, and more often, just plain good American cash.

"I'm like those guys in the books I read in school, just before they kicked me out," thought Patrick. "Just like that Horatio Alger guy. Hell, he could write a book about me, if I can find him," he decided.

A quick sort of his mail had told him that the cities on his itinerary were merely the beginning. Hell, he could make another trip to Rockford, Rock Island and Peoria, plus a dozen other places when he got back from Dubuque, he decided.

Having expected only a half dozen NEA prospects to attend his meeting in an East Dubuque saloon, he was surprised to see the place packed with citizens from not only Dubuque and East Dubuque, but also from Wisconsin, as far away as Platteville and points east. Sam Sladdum, an attorney at the meeting, offered his services to the NEA as legal advisor, and because Patrick had on more than one occasion run afoul of the law, he commissioned Sladdum to represent the budding National Explosives Association, in future litigations, whatever the hell litigations were.

Sladdum explained at the meeting that possessing and carrying explosives were God-given rights, covered by the Second Amendment in the Constitution, explaining how it sanctioned the NEA.

"The right of the people to keep and bear arms shall not be infringed," Sladdum read to the group, directly from the Bill of Rights.

Responses from the tavern audience, all favorable, ranged from "Amen, brother," to "Fuckin' A Right," with a few "Betcher Sweet Ass's", a lone "Right On," from a gray-bearded former flower child, and several "Fuckin' Well Told's" in between.

Sladdum, standing with his arm around Patrick, then explained logically, that in those days, 1791 or something like that, bearing arms referred to muskets, but today, after 200 years of technological improvement, when nations spoke of arms to protect themselves, they sure as shit didn't mean muskets. Arms meant anything that countries spent money for in the arms race, with the bulk of the money being spent on research and development of bigger and better explosives.

"Bigger and better, that's right," said Patrick to himself as he left the toll road to turn north toward O'Hare Airport. And he recalled what was perhaps the most enjoyable part of his Iowa itinerary. It was in Waterloo, where he was welcomed in a fashion similar to the one in East Dubuque, but because some of the Waterloo prospective NEA members had never touched explosives, other than the routine 4th of July blasting of fireworks smuggled in from Missouri and South Dakota, Patrick conducted a half-day workshop on "Explosives Safety," explaining to the receptive audience of 35 men and four women, that it was "damned important, not to get yourself blowed up" when working with dynamite, nitroglycerin, gunpowder packets, or any other type of explosives, that in order to encourage more membership in the NEA, the charter members should practice what he called "Safe Explosives."

"Whenever an NEA member blows himself up," Sladdum had explained to him, "the NEA loses not just one, but perhaps dozens of prospective members, consisting of those youngsters who change their mind about joining when they hear about something like that."

It had all made sense to Patrick, and as he pulled into O'Hare, he chuckled audibly at the crater he had made on a new member's farm, south of Waterloo, where he had conducted the workshop. The lone damage caused by the explosion had been the demolishment of Patrick's red pickup truck, which he had parked a trifle too close to the dynamite.

"Holy shit," the farmer had said, ignoring for a moment the demolished pickup, but focusing instead on the deep crater that had been nothing but swamp land, covered with thistles and mosquitoes, "after a rain or two this hole will fill up with water and we can go fishing here at next fall's meeting. And I want you boys to notice what Mr. O'Shea did to his own pickup, just to demonstrate what happens when you are not careful. It's a damn good thing we wasn't sitting in it, right Mr. O'Shea?"

"Damn right," Patrick had responded, pleased with the compliment and the accompanying applause. And also pleased at being called "Mr.," for that matter.

It was right then that Patrick had felt that pleasant, though of late, not too familiar bulging in the front of his trousers. The only time it previously had happened was when he was either beating up on Hilda or blowing up segments of highway for the state of Illinois. He would have to put on some more workshops, he decided.

"Whenever I do a clean job of blowing up something, I need a woman," Patrick explained to the farmer, who was viewing his crotch with wonder.

"Hot damn," the farmer responded, pointing to the four female NEA prospects, "We'll get you one, take your pick."

"And by God, it had happened," Patrick recalled, as he parked "short term" at the airport. "That very night in Waterloo. All she wanted out of it was a chance to get on one of them talk shows. Told her it had better be that Donahue guy, because the rest of them all sound like foreign sons-a-bitches. And to top it off, she gave me this car from the lot where she works, said it didn't cost her a dime. And here I am, home again."

At the same time Patrick was at O'Hare Airport, thumbing through a pile of newspapers, looking for the story on the dentist's office explosion, Asa was sunning himself in his golf cart, in front of the very office. He loved writing his memoirs on the golf-cart lap computer, having made a copy from the rec room computer and transferring them to his brand-new lap computer. He thought computers were miraculous, lap or otherwise, as he began asking it to find the very same things he had sought on the office computer. "Find Lost Nation," he requested, thinking of one of his two favorite Iowa town names, the other being What Cheer. The computer dutifully responded. "Lost Nation is not found."“

Next, Asa instructed the lap computer to "Find the Cubs in the World Series," to which the computer ruefully answered, "The Cubs in the World Series is not found."

"I think it should be 'are not found,'" Asa told the computer, but to no avail.

Looking up, squinting into the sun, he noticed Inspector Walter O'Kowski watching him, standing with his hand to his jaw and looking disgusted. Not only had he got nowhere in his investigation of Will two days ago, but he had lost his pain pills. He had handwritten a report of the murder plot he had overheard in the bugged rec room, and somewhat against his better judgment, had arranged a meeting with two higher ups in the department, plus an assistant district attorney to disclose his findings.

"OK, make it fast, O'Kowski," Antonio Bassanio had said, looking at his office clock, "What the hell do you want?"

O'Kowski then disclosed his findings at the dental office, while investigating the murder of Muzafer (Gus) Harrigian, telling Bassanio that he had discovered a plot involving two underworld characters named Mario and Luigi who were being sent out to kill Bassanio himself. There was no one else in the whole Chicago police department that could be referred to as "Boss Bass," O'Kowski knowingly informed the trio. But the bad news, O'Kowski informed them, was that Rusty Callahan, his immediate superior on the force, had sneaked into the dental office and was drunkenly bragging about his part in the plot to do away with Bassanio.

All Bassanio had said at the end of the report was, "You know damned well that whoever killed Harrigian had to belong to the Leopold and Loeb fan club, because Gus's skull was found right by the culvert where they dumped Bobbie Franks. Did these Mario and Luigi farts say anything about Leopold and Loeb?" Bassanio asked, winking at his two silent associates.

"I did not observe that in the conversation," admitted O'Kowski.

"Look, O'Kowski," responded Bassanio, indicating by his body language that O'Kowski should get the hell out of there, "You've been working too hard. Take a few days off, with pay, of course, and we will promise to put you on the next case involving a brain surgeon."

"Brain surgeon?" O'Kowski asked, befuddled at the response.

"Yah, you were assigned to that dentist because you had a toothache, right?"

"Yes, Sir, I still have it," said O'Kowski, holding his jaw.

"Then you're the logical one to investigate a brain surgeon suspected of a crime. Now get the fuck out of here and don't bother us. We've got work to do, Asshole."

In front of the office O'Kowski watched Asa on the computer and asked, "What the hell are you doing out here, Old Man? Think you're some kind of reception committee?"

"Can't have only one person on a committee," explained Asa, as O'Kowski ignored his answer.

"What's this 'find' stuff you are looking for on that machine?"

"It is not a machine," said Asa proudly. "It is a Macintosh lap computer. I find things on it. I just ask it to find something and it either does so or informs me that it is not found."

"Well, Old Man, you could make my work a hell of a lot easier if you had that lap computer find the killer of Gus Harrigian."

"I'll try," said Asa, somewhat pleased at the attention he was getting. "How do you spell 'Harrigian'?"

"Try Gus," said O'Kowski, getting more interested by the second.

"Find Gus," Asa typed on the word processor, to which the computer returned the message, "Gus is not found."

"Sorry," said Asa. "Anything else?"

"Just for the hell of it, see if you can find Leopold and Loeb," said O'Kowski, still holding onto his painful jaw, but vaguely recalling his conversation with Bassanio, who somehow believed the crimes were related.

Asa directed his lap computer to find Leopold and Loeb, to which the computer responded with the terms "Leopold and Loeb" highlighted on the screen.

"Son of a bitch," said O'Kowski, admiring the magic. "What else does it say?"

After only two clicks of the mouse on the computer, Asa opened the section titled Leopold and Loeb, where he had typed his memoirs praising the presentation of Randy Harrigan and Will Mosley 25 years before.

"Let's see that," said O'Kowski, knowing he was on to something and forgetting his toothache, as he squinted to read the passage,". . . . . One of the bright spots of my last few years at SUI High was the paired presentation by Randy Harrigan and Will Mosley. Their paper and skit on Leopold and Loeb showed great possibilities, looming far above the caliber of the work of other students. . ."

"Son of a bitch," said O'Kowski. And to himself, "I've heard those names before. Mosley, and Harrigan. Now maybe those bastards downtown will give me a search warrant and listen to me."

"That's really something you've got there," said O'Kowski. "I would like to watch some more. You're pretty good on that machine, but damn, my tooth is still bothering me. Old Man, is Mosley in there torturing some poor son of a bitch? I don't know if I dare go in there or not. He's a real mean bastard, isn't he, Old Man?"

"Really," said Asa. "You must use an adverb to modify an adjective. 'Real' is an adjective. 'Really' is an adverb."

O'Kowski stared at Asa, not knowing what to say, as Asa continued, "You may certainly see him now, he is not too busy today, and most certainly, he will try not to hurt you. There is no need for you to be pusillanimous about seeing a dentist."

"Don't ever call me a pussy lamb's ass, Old man. Watch your goddamned mouth," muttered O'Kowski, holding his jaw and walking around the golf cart through the door to Will's office.

"I'll get these bastards, wait and see," O'Kowski said to himself as he walked in.

This time O'Kowski remained only a few minutes, not even seeing Will, who relayed a new batch of pain pills and penicillin to him. O'Kowski carefully avoided Asa on the way out, vowing to get to the inside of that lap computer for evidence, and proceeded to his unmarked police Buick, where he looked forward to hearing the conversation in the rec room as soon as five o'clock came. And this time he would prove to Bassanio that he had not imagined the mass murder planning of the previous day. He had attached a cassette tape to record every word spoken in the room.

No sound came from the Rec Room until after five o'clock, when Asa got out of his golf cart and walked in, just as Hilda and Will were entering. The conversation at first seemed innocuous to O'Kowski, listening from his car, having to do mostly with a female voice asking someone how he enjoyed the sun. Had to be that old son of a bitch she was talking to, thought O'Kowski, pleased that he was able to make sound deductions, even though those assholes down at the station never could see crimes developing right before their stupid faces.

From there the conversation got suspicious as hell to O'Kowski, as Hilda said, "Get your things together. We're invited out to eat tonight. The boys are back and said they would show us everything we need to know about Mario and Luigi. They said in order to kill the Koopa King, we don't have to wipe out all seven of his kids, but most certainly must destroy Wendy O. Koopa right after we get rid of Boss Bass."

"Holy Jesus," mumbled O'Kowski in his car, "Mother of Mary, Sweet Wenceslaus. They're plotting a mass murder right in front of my goddamned eyes."

He listened intently to, "The boys say after we kill Larry Koopa, Morton, Jr. and Wendy, we can skip Iggy, Roy, Lemmy, and Ludwig von Koopa, and go directly to Bowser, the Koopa King."

"It's that easy?" asked Will, pleased at the prospect of getting away for the evening.

"They say one obstacle is getting rid of the Hammer Brothers in the Dark World," Hilda continued, "They said a black hand comes up and grabs you on the way to Bowser."

In the Police Buick, O'Kowski was thinking, "'Dark World,' I wonder if that's a code word for the south side. And who are the Koopa's? I knew a Wendy Krupa from Cicero a long time ago. Do they mean 'Krupa'? And the 'Black Hand.' That's what they used to call the Mafia before Capone. I'll have to look that up. And it's all on tape. By God, my tooth quit hurting."

As soon as Will wheeled Asa's golf cart into the office, the three of them walked across the parking lot to Will's car, looking forward to being guests of Wolfgang and Max Harrigian. Hilda said she would drive because it wasn't easy to get there if it was your first time.

"Out for supper," said O'Kowski to himself, as he pondered whether to follow them or to stay by the office where he could get hold of Asa's lap computer.

"Hell, I know they'll be back, so I'll just wait. As soon as it gets dark, I'll pay that office a visit. But with the toothache gone, I feel like I could eat first. Wendy Krupa, haven't thought about her for years. Too bad there's a contract on her, but first things first. I'm hungry." So, forgetting Wendy, he drove to the other end of the mall where he found a McDonald's.

At O'Hare Airport, Patrick O'Shea had devoted at least three hours to two tasks, one with which he was very familiar, drinking beer. His other task was much more difficult, reading newspapers. He had given the bar maid a $20 tip to bring him back issues of the Chicago Tribune, and after a few minutes she returned with a whole week's supply of Tribunes, in which he thoroughly expected to see a front-page story and a few follow-ups concerning a big explosion at a nearby dental office. He had read the Dubuque Telegraph Herald and the Waterloo Courier on his NEA organizational trip to Iowa, but had seen nothing about a Chicago explosion, but realized that if the Iowa newspapers published every crime that took place in Chicago, they would have no space at all for local news.

At first, he read only the front pages of the supply of Tribunes, then, seeing no news of the explosion, thumbed through the remainder of each edition, skipping only the sports, comics, want ads, and the huge full-page ads for hardware and convenience stores.

"Shit," muttered Patrick aloud after each unsuccessful search, and "Bring me another Bud," to the barmaid whenever she happened around, which was less and less frequently as the afternoon turned into evening and dusk approached.

His anger at the lack of news transferred to the barmaid, as he staggered out after four beers, commenting, "Next time I come around, I'm gonna beat the piss out of you, Bitch."

The barmaid retreated to the kitchen until Patrick was gone.

Miraculously weaving through traffic off the toll road and into the shopping center, neglecting only to dim his lights when meeting cars, Patrick noticed some evidence that his explosion had gone off as scheduled. There was no blinking neon sign showing from the Chiropractic Clinic.

"Must have blown it up, after all," thought Patrick. "Otherwise, the bone crushers would be busy. It's only 9:00 or so."

What Patrick did not know was that the Clinic turned off its lights and closed two evenings a year, once for the spring commencement exercises at the Palmer College of Chiropractic in Davenport, Iowa, and once again for the summer commencement. The entire staff had taken a chartered bus to Davenport, leaving the shopping center at five p.m.

As Patrick drove close enough to see that the Chiropractic Clinic, lights or no lights, was completely intact, as was the Dental Office, he wondered what had gone wrong. And by God he was going to find out.

Parking his Ford directly in front of the dental office, and remaining in it only long enough to drink two cans of Budweiser for the courage needed to break in to see what went wrong, Patrick checked his keys to see if the office key was still there. It was. As he got out of the car, leaving it unlocked, he looked around, saw only one other car, a Buick, within 100 yards, and prepared to enter the office.

"Hope no son of a bitch steals my car when I'm in there. They might," he said, looking at his rear license. "It's an Iowa plate and Iowa cars don't last long when you park in Illinois."

One would expect a policeman on a stakeout to witness a front-door break-in 40 feet away, but Inspector O'Kowski's pain killer was working, and he was sound asleep, dreaming of retirement with winters in Florida and summers fishing in Wisconsin. The only sound from the rec room, through his speaker was the peaceful and salubrious gurgling of Will's aquarium, perhaps contributing to O'Kowski 's pleasant dreams.

In the office Patrick drunkenly checked one panel in the wall to ascertain whether the dynamite was still there. It was.

"Then why the hell didn't it blow?" said Patrick aloud, waking up O'Kowski, who heard him from his Police Buick.

"What's that?" asked O'Kowski to himself, "they're back already, and it's only, Holy Jesus, I must have gone to sleep, 9:30." He moved his vehicle closer, to within just a few feet of Patrick's Iowa car.

Reading the plates, he said to himself, "I knew it. This crime ring includes the whole damned country. I'll get them for violating the interstate commerce laws."

"God damn contractors," said Patrick to himself. "Selling us duds just to make a buck. Half the shit I stole from the Highway Department is probably worthless. There ought to be a law against that."

"Wonder if the goddamn TV doesn't work," he said aloud, turning it on.

O'Kowski, knowing the conversation was taped, got out of his Buick and stealthily moved toward Will's office. "Sweet Virgin Mother of God," he said, "I can get that lap computer and catch him red-handed at the same time. He's got the whole damned office filled with stolen goods."

"Wonder if I hooked it up to the wrong channel," Patrick asked himself as he switched from Channel 3 to 9.

They were the last words the world ever heard from Patrick O'Shea.

Chapter 13

THE NEWS

The explosion occurred at least an hour too late for the WGN evening news, and even had the commentators mentioned the explosion, neither Will, Asa, nor Hilda would have heard about it. They had spent the entire evening involved in a Nintendo lesson from Wolfgang and Max, with occasional help from their younger brothers, Muzafer, II, six years of age, and Joseph (named after his mother), who mistakenly had thought she would never have a daughter, but now cherished their infant Sally.

At ten o'clock, as Will was thanking Josephine and telling her to give his regards to Randy when she saw him, Josephine said,

"Oh, no. Please stay. We are your hosts. Randy will be home in the morning. He would never forgive me if I let you go."

"I thought he would be here tonight," said Will.

"Oh, I thought you knew. It's his community theatre. Tonight, they are doing Once Upon a Mattress and he decided to sleep there."

"If it is based on 'The Princess and the Pea,'" said Asa, "he'll stay there a long time if he sleeps on a different mattress each night."

"How's that?" Hilda asked.

"Well, now that you asked," said Asa proudly, "the princess slept on 20 mattresses and 20 featherbeds. Under two of them were peas. It was a test to see if she was a true princess. But we'd be happy to spend 40 nights with you, Josephine. You have a wonderful family."

Will interpreted Asa's statement to mean he would like to stay the night at the Harrigians. And Hilda loved baby Sally as much as if she were her own, so they decided to stay, spent another two hours practicing Super Mario 3 with Wolfgang and Max, and retired to their individual guest rooms.

For the first time in weeks, Will slept soundly throughout the night, attributing it to the feeling of protection, almost invincibility, that affected the entire Harrigian household. Perhaps he could get over his skull and corpse obsessions. And perhaps with the help of Randy, he could quit worrying about O'Kowski.

At nine o'clock the next morning, the three guests and the Harrigian family were seated at a huge table, their breakfasts served by two combination butler-body guards, when Randy came bursting into the room carrying an early edition of the Chicago Tribune. Before Will could comment on Randy's lack of disguise, Randy ran over to the three guests, tears in his eyes and individually hugged them.

"Your office blew up last night," he said. "It's in the paper and was on the radio. I was afraid you were dead."

"Randy, is this another joke?" asked Will.

"No, look," said Randy, showing him the headlines. "Front page."

Chiropractic Clinic Explodes

One Believed Dead

"One chiropractic clinic believed dead?" asked Asa, bewildered.

"No, one person," said Randy.

The article went on to say that the elaborate $17 million clinic had been totally demolished, taking with it a nearby dentist's office, destroying beyond recognition two automobiles parked in front, injuring at least one person, plus causing an unknown number of possible fatalities. Police, firemen and various other officials had roped off an area of 400,000 square feet at the scene and were searching for clues in the rubble.

Later in the day, WGN reported that the number of fatalities would have been much higher, had it not been for the commencement exercises at the Palmer College of Chiropractic in Davenport, where the staff had been taken by bus earlier in the day. While police were not disclosing any clues or speculating on the cause of the explosion, one investigator had suggested that foul play was suspected by the police.

That night, still at Randy's home, the adults watched the 9:00 WGN news, hearing the announcer say, "One unidentified survivor, possibly a witness to the explosion, was rushed to Saint Christopher's Hospital in Oak Park. WGN staff will attempt to interview him or her when and if he or she regains consciousness."

"You folks will be here for a while," said Randy apologetically. "We'll get you some clothes and anything else you need and try to keep you as comfortable as possible."

"Thanks," said Hilda. "Josephine offered me some of hers, but they are about three sizes too small."

"Tell Josephine your sizes and we'll fix you up. What about you Asa?"

"I have nothing, need nothing," said Asa, "if my golf cart and lap computer survived the explosion."

"They didn't," said Randy, jotting "golf cart" and "lap computer" on a piece of paper.

Two days later, wearing new clothes as they sat in front of the television, the five adults heard the announcer say that the one fatality in the explosion had been identified by dental forensic scientists as Willard Mosley, 43, formerly of Elmhurst, but more recently residing in nearby motels. Mosley was preceded in death by his mother and father. His lone survivor, recently separated wife Karen, was believed to be living in Memphis, but could not be located. The couple had no children "that we know of," the announcer concluded cautiously.

"You're dead," said Randy, grinning at Will.

"How about us?" Asa asked.

"We'll have to wait and see," said Randy.

The next day, Randy had one of his men bring in some Iowa newspapers, particularly those from Iowa City and Cedar Rapids, both of which published individual stories, adding what is known as local color to news items. The Cedar Rapids Gazette announced in a small headline, "Former Iowa Native Killed," which Asa pondered over for some time before saying, "I want to call them up. A native of any place is always a native. There are no former natives. Jesus was, is, and always will be a native of Bethlehem because he was born there. And the same goes for Will and Iowa."

Randy explained to Asa that all outgoing calls had to go through the switchboard, which was badly in need of repair. In other words, the phones in the Harrigian home were temporarily out of order.

Somehow, the Iowa City Press Citizen staff knew the contents of Willard Mosley's Last Will and Testament and explained that he had willed his body to the University of Iowa Hospitals, but that for no more body than they had been able to find, merely a fragment or two of skull and most of his teeth, the Hospital would probably hand his remains over to the University of Iowa Dental School.

That evening, while Hilda and Asa were playing Nintendo, Will and Randy were watching the news when Will heard the announcer say, "Possible witness of the explosion." He looked at the screen fearfully, not because he himself had anything to do with the explosion, but because his other deeds remained on his conscience. The camera shifted to a hospital room in St. Christopher's Hospital, where a reporter was attempting to interview Walter O'Kowski. Also in the room was O'Kowski 's chief or commander (Will did not know which and neither did the reporter). But the higher-up's name was Antonio Bassanio of the Chicago Police Force.

"What happened, Mr. O'Kowski?" asked the reporter. O'Kowski 's face was completely covered with bandages except for the end of his nose and most of his mouth, which was enough for Will to believe it truly was Walter O'Kowski.

"Toothache," mumbled O'Kowski. "Dentist fixed it. Didn't even have an appointment. Took a nap in my car after the pain killer started working, woke up later, got out of the car to stretch before going home. And the next thing I remember I was here in your studio."

"It's a hospital, Mr. O'Kowski" the reporter said, looking at Bassanio.

"We are having a citation made up for Walter O'Kowski," said Bassanio. "He is indeed a hero, but he really doesn't know any more about what happened than you do. He's been working a lot of overtime lately. Good man. He will spend the rest of the summer fishing in Wisconsin, if he recovers, which, speaking on behalf of the department, I certainly hope he does."

At the Harrigian house, Will said, "Glad he's still alive."

"Even if you're dead?" chuckled Randy. "Are you going to your funeral?"

"No, I'll take a raincheck," said Will. "Tell me, what should we do, really?"

"Well, how much do you still owe the government?"

"About $250,000," said Will. "Plus interest."

"We have documented proof that you are dead. And you have no heirs, no estate. You gave Hilda your Power of Attorney, your money is withdrawable by number, not by name. No way will the government get any money from you. Aren't you really better off dead?"

"What happens to people after they die . . . when they are still alive?" asked Will. "You know at least two now. I'm one. Your father-in-law is another. Where can we go? What do we do?"

"Every year a lot of people who know too much have their identities changed by the FBI. Entire families are whisked away in the night. That TV program where that zombie stiff-legs his way to the front of the screen and talks about unsolved mysteries will last forever, because they find only about one missing person of every fifty, and the number is growing."

"Which number?" asked Will.

"You're sounding more like Asa every day," said Randy. "The fifty, or whatever the hell number I said. And don't worry about Muzafer. He's fine. You'll be visiting him after things settle down here."

"But what about Hilda and Asa, and your own family? What do they do when they find that someone who is supposed to be dead is really alive? What do we tell them?" Will wanted to know.

"Will, I'll tell you something. Our family has no secrets from one another. Josephine, Wolfgang and Max talked this over before Muzafer's funeral. They know he is OK, but Josephine keeps things to herself. And the kids inherited this quality, just as they did Muzafer's pointed teeth. They know more than you think."

Will had a final question, "But what do we tell Hilda and Asa?"

"Look, they're both happier than they have been in years. They know you are alive, that's for damned sure, and they know you are passing for dead. Asa himself told me this morning that having you alive while pretending to be dead is far superior to having you dead, while pretending you are alive. Says that was what happened to him in the Care Center. Dead but pretending to be alive."

Will nodded, trying to take in Randy's explanation, not really surprised that Hilda and Asa, the two people in the world who meant more to him than anyone else, with the possible exception of Randy, knew more than they had let on.

"And as for the rest of the world," Randy continued, "about half the people I run into at the community theatre say they have been born again, and they are damned proud of the fact."

"Born again?" asked Will.

"Yah, born again Christians, . . . they don't look any younger, but they feel a hell of a lot better and go out and spread the word, trying to get new converts. Hell, this place you went to find Karen, the Elvis Presley mansion?"

"Yes?" asked Will.

"Most of them have been born again, or at least they say they have been, which amounts to the same thing. The only way you and my father-in-law differ from the Presley people is that you and Gus don't brag about being born again. You're damned quiet about it. Make sense to you, Will?"

It did indeed make sense to Will. No wonder Randy had risen so high in AAAA. He knew how to talk to people, Will said to himself. And he knows everything.

Will had one or two final items to clear up before deciding on his future. First, even though the teeth of Patrick O'Shea had been identified as his own, would anyone miss Hilda's legal husband, and if so, what would they do about it?

The other question concerned the future of his own wife, Karen. She said she was filing for divorce. Was it final? Could Randy find out?

The next day three of Randy's combination research assistant-body guards handed Randy three news clippings, one two weeks old, the other two, from yesterday's newspaper editions.

A copy of the August 1, Memphis Elvis Presley Banner included a brief item with a mysterious one-word headline, "Defenestration."

The two paragraph-item read, "Deborah Barker, formerly Karen Mosley, and now widow of the late Reverend Billy Bob Barker, died on impact yesterday when she leaped from an upstairs window of the Elvis Presley Mansion.

"Ms. Barker, a tour bus driver for the Presley Memorial Museum, was observed stepping over a rope, sealing off the upstairs from tourists, and climbing up the stairs to the top floor, where she (along with many others) believed Elvis to be living. One moment later, after her defenestration, her lifeless body was found on the ground beneath a second-floor window. Mourning her death was a small poodle, seen at the window, barking frantically."

At the Harrigian mansion, Randy asked Will, "What's defenestration?" to which one of the combination research assistant-body guards responded, "Death by being thrown through a window. If she jumped of her own volition, the term 'defenestration' is used incorrectly. And the poodle seen in the window could not possibly have thrown her out."

"I'll be damned," said Randy, complimenting his research assistant-body guard, "you could have taught with Asa at SUI High."

For a few moments the room was silent as Will sat dumfounded, tears in his eyes, wondering how he could have saved his marriage and consequently Karen's life.

The other two news items, one from the Waterloo Courier, the other from the Dubuque Telegraph Herald, concerned the newly formed National Explosives Association and a stolen Ford. New members of the NEA had apparently been bilked by organizer Patrick O'Shea, who had taken their money and the car, fleeing to Canada or Mexico with the loot.

"So," asked Randy after Will had digested the news items, "what next? I suggest you join my father-in-law."

"Not without Hilda and Asa," responded Will.

"Of course," agreed Randy.

Chapter 14

THE NEW REPUBLIC

Josephine Harrigian insisted that the three guests have a good breakfast before departing on an AAAA helicopter to its special landing berth at the Milwaukee airport, where they boarded a new AAAA jet, which whisked them to the airport at Yerevan, capital city of the former Soviet Socialist Republic of Armenia. But now, since the dissolution of the Soviet Union, Armenia had become a newly independent, autonomous, though landlocked nation. Additionally, Yerevan itself, in the past few months had set up its own government, claiming 1001 square miles of the former Armenian Soviet Socialist Republic as its own, making it smaller than Rhode Island, but larger by seven square miles than Kossuth County, the largest in Iowa and larger by three square miles than Chicago's Cook County.

It was without exaggeration to say that AAAA, Ltd. had played an important role in Yerevan's independence, which Will was soon to see for himself.

Upon arriving, they were cordially welcomed by Muzafer Harrigian's combination customs official-bodyguards, who had been processing new identification documents for Will, Hilda and Asa. Muzafer (Gus) Harrigian made an unaccustomed appearance at the scene a few minutes later, embraced and kissed the three newcomers, telling them, "Just like me. You will be born again."

"First thing, name change. Should end in 'ian' so we fit in with crowd," said Gus, "Armenian names end in 'ian.' What name you want?"

"Christian ends with 'ian'," said Will, attempting to maintain at least a semblance of his past life, "I want to be called 'Christian.'"

"Okay," said Gus to the chief customs official-bodyguard, "This is Christian. Write down 'Christian.'"

"Christian?" asked the official. And repeating, just to make certain, "Christian?"

"Yes," said Will, "My name is Christian Christian." And looking at Hilda and Asa, he asked, "Is Christian OK for you?"

"Holy Jesus," said Hilda, happily, "are you proposing? It's about time, thank God."

"Yes," said Will, putting his arm around Hilda. "I want you to take my Christian name."

Listening carefully, Asa asked, "Is Christian your Christian name? Or is it your surname? I think Hilda should have a different Christian name."

"Yes," agreed Will. And to Hilda, "What do you want for a first name?"

Hilda thought for a moment and responded, "Anastasia. Anastasia Christian," to which the combination customs-official bodyguard dutifully typed 'Anastasia Anastasia Christian' as her identity.

"And you?" Asa was asked by the official.

"First name will be Bjorn, spelled B J O R N," said Asa. "and for a middle name, spell it 'A G I A N' but pronounced 'again,' resulting in the complete name 'Bjorn Agian Christian.'" And to Will he said, "A lot of the students at SUI high spelled 'again' improperly, reversing the two middle vowels."

With their new identification papers, and names quite easy to remember, the three had dinner with Muzafer Harrigian that evening, who told them they could live with him or anywhere else in the new Armenia Republic, and as soon as he got a few things ironed out, they could visit the United States any time they wished, without fear of being arrested.

"How's that?" Will asked.

"We're working on membership in the United Nations. Since the breakup of the Soviet Union, they have been taking in everybody. What would you rather be, Ambassador to the United States or our delegate to the United Nations? Either way you will be in your native land, and also you will have diplomatic immunity."

"Do we have to decide now?" asked Will, amazed at the turn of events.

"Take your time, Christian," said Muzafer. "Randy tells me you and Anastasia probably want your own family. If that's what you want, stay here and," (looking at Asa) "we can give either job to Bjorn Agian if he wants one."

"I want only a couple of things," said Bjorn Agian, smiling at Muzafer.

"What's that?"

"No, what are those?" corrected Bjorn Agian.

"Tell him what you want," Anastasia pleaded.

"Not much, a golf cart, lap computer, and a Nintendo set with a Super Mario III game."

"In the next room," said Muzafer.

"As for you," said Muzafer, looking to the other two. "You had better get busy on that family." And, looking at his watch, added, "It's getting late."

The End

Made in USA - Crawfordsville, IN
15770_9798533860574
08.11.2021 1724